I0571917

Oh
Brother
A Novel

CHRISTY POTTER

Other Books by Christy Potter

The World Was My Oyster But I Didn't Know How to Cook

Recipient of the Princeton Literary Review's Gold Standard for Literary Excellence, this book offers Christy's best humorous and thought-provoking essays on New York (her adopted home), Kansas (where she's from), childhood, books, infertility, good days, bad days, and life in general, as well as interviews she has done with well-known writers like Janet Evanovich and Lois Lowry. Acclaimed author P.F. Kluge calls this book "A lively mix of words...and life."

The Shiksa's Guide to Yiddish

A definitive collection of Yiddish words and phrases specifically for non-Jewish women who marry Jewish men. Written from the point of view of a woman who has done just that, each word includes a pronunciation guide along with the definition, and usually an anecdote from Christy's own life. Between chapters are witty observations on Jewish life through the eyes of a shiksa who has embraced the Jewish people wholeheartedly.

Copyright © 2013 by Christy Potter Kass

All rights reserved.
No part of this publication may be reproduced, distributed, or transmitted in any form or by any means, including photocopying, recording, or other electronic or mechanical methods, without the prior written permission of the publisher, except in the case of brief quotations embodied in critical reviews and certain other noncommercial uses permitted by copyright law. For permission requests, write to the publisher, addressed "Attention: Permissions Coordinator," at the address below.

Top Down Publishing
P.O. Box 636
Convent Station, NJ 07961

http://www.ChristyTheWriter.com

Ordering Information:Quantity sales. Special discounts are available on quantity purchases by corporations, associations, and others. For details, contact the publisher at the address above.

Published in the United States of America

Publisher's Cataloging-in-Publication dataPotter, Christy Oh Brother, A Novel

ISBN 978-0-9891651-5-0 Main category —Contemporary. 2. Family Life 3. Humorous. 4. Romance General

Author Potter, Christy. Oh Brother, A Novel

Print Edition

Dedicated to first wives everywhere

There have been three times in my life when people told me, right to my face, that I was crazy. The first was when I dropped out of college and moved into a sustainable human biosphere in northern California, the second was when I divorced my hugely successful software developer husband, and the third was when I married his hippie artist brother.

Granted, the only person who told me that I was crazy for that whole biosphere thing was my father, and the only one who told me I was crazy when I married the artist was my ex-husband. Still, it's hard to be told you're crazy, especially when you sometimes wonder if they might be right.

Zen and the Art of Stealing Fig Newtons

Born and raised in San Francisco, I'm an only child, christened Ariel Blanche Carson, daughter of Susan and Earl Carson, parents who were average everything except for uptightness, at which they were off the charts. They regulated everything I ate, everything I watched on TV, what time I went to bed, what time I got up, what friends I had, even how much "leisure time" I was allowed every day, and even that was regimented to the point that I played with certain toys and games on specific days so they could be sure I was getting the right stimulus and mental challenges. While I didn't know it for a fact, I suspected my name was selected so the initials were orderly. ABC. God.

Then one day when I was six, I came home from school and my mother put me at the kitchen table. She opened a new package of Fig Newtons and put three on my plate, as usual, along with a half-cup of two percent milk, then went into the bathroom, cut off all her hair with a nail scissors, took the rest of the package of Fig Newtons, got into her car and drove away. We never saw her again.

It was a good time explaining that to my father when he got home from work. For months he tried to sort out what had gone wrong, why she'd left without a word, where she'd gone, and how he could have fixed it before it broke. What I kept returning to in my child's mind was why she'd taken the Fig Newtons. They were the only treat I was allowed, and she'd taken them with her. For the first few years after she left, I told myself she didn't love me enough to be my mother anymore, and took the rest of my cookies just to prove it to me. By the time I was in college and had sat through a couple of psychology courses, I concluded that she took the Fig Newtons as she was walking out of our lives as a symbolic act of breaking out of a prison – a prison of her own making – and simultaneously attempting to fulfill a deep-seated and unnamed hunger inside her with the very treat she had so strictly rationed out to her child. Now that I'm in my 40s, I think she was just nuts.

I'm pretty sure my entire regimented childhood is the reason I always bring home all manner of creature comforts. My house is less of a house and more of a nest, feathered with all kinds of pillows and cushions, candles, tapestries, oil paintings, figurines, music and cookbooks and fuzzy slippers and a huge bolt of raw silk I bought on an impulse once during a trip to Asia just because I liked the way it felt against my skin. As a sculptor, I can only function creatively when I'm surrounded by these things that to others may seem like clutter but to me are tiny, tangible Muses that make my soul sing. Also I eat Fig Newtons compulsively. I crave them. I have one cupboard in my house that is always stocked. Trite, yeah. I know. But they are good with coffee.

Fortunately, my husband understands. He's pretty Zen about everything. I mean my second husband, of course. My first husband wasn't Zen about anything.

When Buffalo Whistling-Wind Met Soaring Dove

I was a junior at UCLA when I dropped out and moved to a community near Big Sur that had been organized a few years earlier as an experiment in living completely self-contained. They grew their own food, handled their own waste disposal (you don't want to know), had no phones, no computers, no real address, no electricity, and considered themselves completely separate from the laws that governed California and, most especially, the rest of the country. They called themselves a "sustainable human biosphere," and while I'm not sure they really knew what they meant by that, their ideas and practices were something I felt I could get behind.

I had become quite a radical free spirit by this point in my life, ready to try anything that made me feel unencumbered. The idea of this community being completely off the grid appealed to me in a way that was almost primal. From the moment I heard about it, I pined for it, obsessed over it, until one day I packed up my dorm room, loaded everything into my ancient, tiny pickup truck and stopped at the registrar's office on my way out of town to tell them I was quitting school.

"You had a scholarship," my father said when I called him from a gas station pay phone on the way to Big Sur. "You had a full scholarship to UCLA. And you dropped out? You're not dropping out, Ariel. Go back."

"I'm not going back, Dad, I need to do this."

"You won't get anywhere in the world without a college degree."

"I can think about two dozen people right off the top of my head who have proved that false."

"They're the exception, not the rule, and you know that."

"I'm not having this argument with you, Dad. I'm going. This is my life and I'm running it now."

"You're crazy."

"Yes," I said. "Yes, I probably am. Must run in the family."

I lived in the biosphere for two years, and I loved it. Unlike the communes you see in movies about the 60s, we didn't run around topless all the time – only on holidays and special occasions – and we didn't have free love and naked babies all over the place that everyone raised together. We did smoke a lot of weed, though. We gave ourselves Native American-sounding names, and we gardened and wrote and read and played music and swam in the ocean, and we'd regularly have community meetings where we'd sit around the fire pit that served as the center of our village, and pass around the communal pipe and talk about how awesome it was to not be a part of the possession-and-wealth driven world outside and how much that whole thing sucked, man.

I didn't get involved with any of the men in the community, for no reason other than none of them appealed to me in anything other than a brotherly kind of way. I did make friends with a girl from Idaho named Lisa Wentworth. The night we were sitting around the fire, taking turns announcing the Native American names we had chosen for ourselves, we got to her and she said "Lemon Wax" in a way that made me suspect she'd forgotten what we were talking about and just said the first two words that popped into her head when she saw that everyone's eyes were on her. She is sweet and fragile and kind of spacey, so no one had the heart to tell her that Lemon Wax, while no doubt a good way to make your furniture nice and shiny, is a damned stupid name. We're still best friends, and to this day, I call her Lem. By now, it just sort of suits her.

The community's utopia was shattered when Buffalo Whistling-Wind (real name Eric Leibowitz), the community's founder, was spotted walking out of a Best Buy in Carmel with six CDs and a car phone by Soaring Dove (real name Marilyn Wagner), his on-and-off love interest, who was sneaking over to Payless Shoes for their BOGO sale. This led to a major screaming match over who was spying on who, and who was indulging in blatant consumerism that was a real slap in the face to everything the community had worked to overcome, and who cares, she never trusted him anyway, not since she caught him looking too long at Wildflower Running Deer while she was weeding the garden without a shirt on.

So the community fell apart and we all went our separate ways. I went back to UCLA and picked up my studies again, sans scholarship, which made my father madder than when I dropped out in the first place. On my first night back in the dorm, I unpacked, ate an entire package of Fig Newtons, and slept for 19 hours. On my second day back, I met Ralph. I'd have been better off if I'd stayed asleep.

Ralph the Magnificent

Ralph is the human equivalent of curb appeal. He looks good from a distance, all shiny windows and smooth lawn, but once you move in, you find out the roof leaks, there are rats in the basement and something stinks. We met in an art history class. I was taken by his quick smile and easy laugh. He's also intelligent and well-spoken, but I was probably the most enraptured by the fact that he wore perfectly pleated slacks and dress shirts with the sleeves rolled up. After two years of men in earth shoes and hemp pants, which I'd liked at the time, it was a refreshing change to look at the kind of guy who you just knew was going to smell like CK One and spearmint gum.

We got married two months after graduation, in a lavish ceremony that was much more him than me, but I didn't mind, mostly because he planned the whole thing and all I had to do was find a dress and show up. He'd already landed a job as a software developer in Silicon Valley and wanted to show off his nice fat paycheck. I was working part time at the public library and spending the rest of my time sculpting, wondering if I'd ever be good enough for a real show. Even if I never was, I truly loved doing it. Sometimes it was the only thing that saved what there was of my sanity.

Some of my friends questioned my decision to marry Ralph. I guess they could see something I couldn't, or maybe wasn't willing to. I couldn't even tell them why I wanted to marry him, and I'm pretty sure it's because I didn't. But I also couldn't think of a good reason not to, and I was getting perilously close to 30, that number that somewhere along the way was branded into women's brains in indelible ink, always there to remind us that if we want to get married and have children, we'd better hurry up. We like to believe we've evolved enough to stop thinking of unmarried women over 30 as old maids, but except for a handful of well-adjusted young women raised by equally well-adjusted mothers, most of us still do. The expiration date that nature has stamped onto our eggs doesn't help matters either.

It sounds like I'm blaming societal pressure for my decision to marry the wrong man, and maybe I am. It's easier than admitting I screwed up. But at any rate, I married Ralph. He bought a beautiful old Victorian house in San Francisco's Alamo Square as a wedding gift to me. It wasn't what I'd have chosen, had he consulted me, but from my tiny attic studio, I could see the tops of the Golden Gate and Bay bridges, and the neighborhood was nice and relatively quiet.

Ralph and I were happily married for about eight minutes. He has a terrible temper and was very controlling. You'd think I'd be used to that because of the way I was raised, but this was different. In the first place, I wasn't a kid anymore, and second, Ralph's continual hissy fits made it hard to take anything he said seriously.

It also didn't take long before he realized he didn't like living with a sculptor because I used clay and wood, both messy, and because I sometimes stopped a project halfway through and left it while I started something else. I always went back to whatever I'd left and finished it when I was ready, but to Ralph, my entire way of working was chaos, madness, and the epitome of everything that was wrong with me, with women, with Democrats, and with everyone else in the world who wasn't him. He also hated my Muses, which he called garage-sale crap, and made fun of my stockpile of Fig Newtons. We fought all the time. Or rather, Ralph fought. I hate fighting so I'd just try to ignore him as best I could until his hurricane of bullshit blew itself out.

He regularly told me I was useless, stupid, and completely void of artistic talent. His favorite old saw was "If you think you're ever going to make it as an artist, you're even stupider than I thought." If we'd dated longer before we got married, I like to think I'd have realized he had such a short fuse and that marrying him would be a colossal, epic mistake. Good old hindsight.

I learned to just tune him out most of the time, but once in awhile I'd fire back at him and then things would really get ugly. Freedom of Speech only applies to Ralph, you see. The corner of the attic I'd claimed as my studio became my refuge more and more. I loved that space, with its angled windows and slanted ceiling. I'd decorated it with an old throw rug I'd gotten at a thrift store for six dollars, a couple of wooden chairs I'd rescued from the garbage and repainted, my tiny CD player, a framed poster of Brancusi sitting cross-legged and smoking a cigarette, and various old wooden tables and stands that were covered in an array of dried clay splatters and my tools, which I kept in old terra cotta flower pots when I could remember to actually put them away. My studio was my sanctuary, my hidey-hole, the place I'd run to when I needed to get away from Ralph or the bills or just life. Brancusi would watch me, his angular face stern beneath his wild beard and hair, his hand holding a cigarette, absolutely still, waiting for me to finish a line or an eye or an angle.

When we weren't fighting, Ralph would go into Super Husband mode, bringing me flowers, candy, jewelry, bottles of expensive perfume he liked. Just when I'd start to think maybe things were going to be okay, a switch would flip and I'd find myself at the business end of his verbal gun. Eventually, I just shut down. I went through the motions, focusing on my work and my life outside of him, finding excuses to be out of the house as much as possible, waiting until he was asleep to go to bed.

Not that he really noticed that part of it. At its best, our sex life was something out of a sixth grade health class film strip. If it wasn't for Geoffrey, my trusty old vibrator, my vagina would have just grown shut like when you first get your ears pierced and accidentally leave the hypoallergenic studs out for too long.

"You seem unhappy," Lem told me one day when I was lamenting my life. "I can sense it."

I'd just told her I was unhappy, but she always wanted a psychic ability she didn't have, so she'd repeat what she'd just been told, or something really obvious, and then smile to herself, amazed and awed at her gift.

"I am unhappy," I said. "But I know it's not as bad as some women have it. Besides, he is good looking and successful."

In my own mind, I knew I was just too lazy to leave and start all over again. Besides, I liked his family. His parents were nice, I was close with his sister, and his brother, Sanford, was proving to be a great ally when it came to my work. He was also an artist – a painter who works exclusively in oils. What he works on is not nearly so limited as I've seen him paint on canvas, cardboard, plywood, his hightop sneakers and once, after a bottle of homemade dandelion wine, on an empty potato chip bag.

I liked Sandy. He worked at The Somerfield, an art gallery nearby, and would often pop in to see how my work was going. He was always telling Ralph to lighten up, that I'm an artist and artists know how they need to work, and if Ralph kept trying to shove my round peg into his square hole, he'd kill my creative spirit. This would have worked, I'm sure, except for the fact that Ralph thinks Sanford is an even bigger flake than I am, so he dismissed anything his brother said as the ravings of a lunatic.

His respect for me wasn't any higher, which is why I'm surprised I was surprised the day he announced he didn't want to be married to me anymore.

Joy to the Fishes in the Deep Blue Sea

Two weeks after I moved out and into a tiny studio apartment in Ashbury Heights, Ralph called my cell phone.

"Are you done pouting? Are you ready to come home?"

"Oh my God, are you serious?"

"Yes, I'm serious. You've had your little snit, now it's time for you to come home."

"Ralph, do you know where you've called me?"

"What?"

"My apartment, Ralph. My new apartment. My new home. I live here now. This is my home."

"What are you saying, Ariel?"

"I'm saying I'm not coming home because I am home. You're the one who said you didn't want to be married anymore."

"Oh come on. I say stuff when I'm angry but I never really mean it. You should know that by now."

"There are a lot of things I should have known by now," I said. "I'm not coming back. Not now. Not ever."

I ended the call and sat for a moment, hands shaking. I looked up at Brancusi. He held my eyes for a long moment while I felt the wave of what I had to do swelling inside of me. Then it crested. I reached for the phone book the last tenant had left behind, called the first lawyer whose number was listed in the yellow pages, and told her I wanted to file for divorce. Then I cried.

To this day, I'm not sure I understand why I was crying. I didn't love Ralph anymore – by that point I was pretty sure I had never loved him in the first place. I didn't miss him, I didn't want to be with him, and I didn't regret moving out. I just felt cheated, abandoned, deceived, and mad as hell.

I stayed in bed, alternately crying and sleeping, for three days. On the third day, Lem showed up with six pints of Ben and Jerry's Cherry Garcia.

"Six pints?" I asked, after blowing my nose. "Why did you get so much?"

"Because I thought seven might be too many," she answered, smiling gently as she floated into the kitchen to get spoons. Stuff that almost makes sense to most people always makes complete sense to Lem.

She made a living writing self-published books of poetry that no one really understood but bought and read fanatically because they almost made sense. Lem drove her readers batty trying to read between the lines of her poems, striving to understand her, struggling in vain to reach whatever plane she is on. They couldn't know, bless their little cotton socks, that no one could achieve Lem's plane of reality because it didn't actually exist. Planet Lem: Population 1.

As I lay on my bed, eyes stinging and hot from so much crying, I watched her dance around the kitchen with her light little fairy steps, and found myself comforted just having her nearby. Her gauzy dress was, as it usually was, a pale yellow. At some point recently she had dyed her hair bright pink. She is a natural blonde, but she was constantly dying it some otherworldly color. In my overwhelmingly fragile emotional state, I suddenly found it endearing. She came back with the spoons and we sprawled side by side and ate ice cream right out of the container until we were almost sick.

"Are you excited?" she asked, digging out a big piece of chocolate.

"About what? The looming specter of an ugly divorce? The financial drain of a lawyer? The fact that six people I thought were my friends said I was crazy for divorcing a husband who is so successful? Having to start my life over again at 35?"

Lem looked at me incredulously.

"Having to start over? Are you loopy? Are you out of your mind?"

Always a disconcerting question out of her.

"Why?"

"First of all, you're not starting your life again. You had a full, rich, wonderful life before you met Randy."

"Ralph."

"Yes. And second of all, you don't have to make a new start, you get to. Not everyone gets the chance to start again."

"I thought you said I wasn't starting again," I said, disagreeably.

"You said you were starting your life again. You're not starting your life again. You're starting new from here. From right now. It's like if you're driving down the road and your car stalls. You call someone to come and jump the battery, you don't push it all the way back home and start the trip all over."

I wasn't ready for Lem to make sense. I started to cry again, knowing she was right, but still feeling a sense of loss and failure. She put her arms around me and rocked me like a baby while I sobbed. She began to sing, in a soothing, motherly voice.

"Jeremiah was a bullfrog…was a good friend of mine… never understood a single word he said, but I helped him drink his wine."

"Are you singing Three Dog Night?" I asked, my face still buried against her shoulder.

"Mm hm," she said, still rocking me.

"Uh, why?"

"Would you rather I sing something else?" she asked. I sat up and looked at her, at her sweet, blank, Kewpie doll face, and I started to laugh. She stared back at me for a moment, then she laughed too. We laughed until we were exhausted, then started to sing again.

"Joy to the world… all the boys and girls now… joy to the fishes in the deep blue sea. Joy to you and me!"

Out with the Old, in with the New

The divorce was quick, but not painless as Ralph was determined to drag it out as long as possible to make me suffer and pay me back for "abandoning him." I pointed out that he had been the one who said he didn't want to be married, but I might as well have been talking to the wall. Whenever he had an audience, he would give a Shakespeare-worthy soliloquy about his faithless wife who had deserted him when all he had asked her for was a little time to clear his thoughts so he could be sure of his love. And thou, o heartless wench, didst not return my ardor and left me a broken and lifeless man! Whither and woe!

I, having made the decision that it was over, was eager to be done with it and move on with my life. I steeled my backbone and managed to withstand every onslaught by Ralph and his oily lawyer, every late night drunken phone call from Ralph, crying and telling me he missed me, every angry email calling me a fat whore, every mediation meeting in which Ralph alternately glared at me and tried to flirt with me. Divorcing him was proving to be more exhausting than being married to him, and that's really saying something.

Lem went with me the day it was finalized, as I really didn't want to face Ralph alone. Turns out there was no need as neither he nor his lawyer even showed up. When the judge's gavel hit the desktop and he proclaimed me divorced, it was all I could do not to hurl myself at him and kiss him right on the mouth. Lem and I went out for a three-martini lunch to celebrate, and after that my life settled into a quiet peacefulness that I thoroughly enjoyed. I'd expected to feel off balance and lonely, but I quickly learned there's a difference between being lonely and being alone.

As I unpacked all my knickknacks, all my creature comforts, and found places for them in my new home, I began to feel more settled and gradually I was at peace again. There, ensconced in my nest, I felt safe.

The really interesting part is that I never realized I didn't feel safe before. Ralph, for all his faults, never laid a hand on me, so the physical threat that drives women to leave abusive relationships wasn't there. If he'd hit me, I'd have known I wasn't safe and would have split before he'd even unclenched his fist. But his assaults were verbal, emotional, and the bruises didn't show. I didn't know I hadn't felt safe until I was gone. The first time I came home to my new apartment after work, the relief that greeted me was palpable.

Sanford showed up one day to ask my opinion about a painting he'd done. In true Sanford form, he didn't call first or even knock, he just came in, somehow managing to bump his painting into both sides of the doorway in the process so that two muffled clunks and three swear words heralded his arrival.

"Does this suck?" he demanded, holding the painting up in such a way that I had the urge to run through it, like a high school football player at the opening game.

"No," I said. "And you know it doesn't. What's the matter?"

"Since when do you listen to critics?" I picked up a fork from the little table beside me and speared a Fig Newton with it. It was a trick I'd learned ages ago to keep from eating clay.

"Since always. A good artist must absorb criticism and use it to better himself, to grow as an artist." He flopped down on the sofa.

"Wow, that's the biggest load of crap I've ever heard out of you, and I've heard plenty."

"I've decided to turn over a new artistic leaf," he said, hoisting himself up and going to the refrigerator for a beer. "Are you busy?"

I held up my clay-covered hands. "Yes."

"Well, do you want to go out with me?"

I frowned at the clay in front of me, turning it a little so I could see better.

"What?" I asked, distracted.

"Sorry, bit of a non sequitur. What I meant to say was, if you're not busy tonight and would like to wash the clay off your hands, I'd be honored to take you out to dinner."

"You mean, like a date?"

"Yes, something like that."

"Something like that? Or like that?"

"Like that."

"You're asking me out?"

"Well I was, but now I'm thinking you might be too much hassle."

"Wow, okay… yes."

"Yes?"

"Yes."

"You're sure? It's only taken you two and half hours to answer me. I want you to be sure."I laughed."Yes. Yes, I will have dinner with you."

He leaned over and kissed me. I was too surprised to even react at first, although later I noticed clay fingerprints on the back of his shirt, so I must have reacted more than I realized.

We went to dinner. A month later, we got married.

If it's Not One Thing, it's Your Brother

With Sandy, I found a happiness I never knew existed, much less hoped to ever feel. We bought a cute little townhouse with a small yard. We adopted a dog from the shelter, an ancient yellow lab named Roscoe who was blind in one eye, had arthritic hips, and thought he was a lap dog. I planted flowers, Sandy mowed the lawn on Saturday afternoons. The studio I created in the spare bedroom was bright and sunny, and I hung my art prints on the wall, Brancusi in the middle, and spent many hours creating in perfect bliss. Days blended into weeks, months, years. Sandy and I co-existed peacefully, working on our art, holding hands wherever we went, spooning at night. It wasn't so much the blissful, giddy days of new love, it was more like relaxing into the comfort of the way it was supposed to be. I felt I'd always been with him, and he with me. Somewhere along the way, our souls had gotten separated but now, in this life, we'd found each other again.

And then Ralph moved in with us.

Yeah, I didn't see that coming either. And don't think I didn't fight it, because I fought it like a cat in the bath. I would have anyway, but Ralph's calling every single one of our former couple friends after he'd heard I was dating Sandy and telling them that I'd left him because I'd been having a secret, long-term affair with his brother made me want to stab him in the eye with a rusty butter knife. Hard.

But Sandy is a gentle soul, a trusting sort, and when Ralph called him up with a sob story about how his girlfriend had thrown him out (even changed the locks – I was so impressed) and the very next day he was laid off from his job and was spending his last quarter to call his favorite brother from a pay phone on his way to warm his hands around the ol' oil drum with the other homeless people under that bridge downtown, Sandy insisted he stay with us until he got back on his feet.

Super.

In our room that first night, Sanford bobbed and weaved around a barrage of angry whispers I pelted at him. How could he do this to me? How could he force me to live under the same roof with my ex-husband? How could he have no respect for me? How could he ask me to endure the very hell I had extricated myself from at great personal cost?

"He's my brother," he said, kissing me, as though that settled it.

"Sandy!" I protested in a shrill whiny voice I didn't even recognize. Roscoe came over and leaned against my leg, protective for six seconds before lying down and beginning to snore.

"Babe, it's not forever. It's just for a little while until he gets another job." He took my hand. "I know you have a good heart and you wouldn't really want me to turn my own brother away when he's in such a bad place."

"Oh, fine," I relented. "But only because I love you. Because I hate him."

"You don't hate," he corrected me. "Never hate another human being." He launched into a horribly off-key rendition of "I'd Like to Teach the World to Sing." Roscoe got up and left the room. I got into bed and piled all the pillows over my head. How come every time I built a happy little world around me, it managed to find a way to fall apart?

A Pathetic Little Gnat's Ass by Any Other Name…

Breakfast that first morning was quite an adventure.

"Good morning, and how's my favorite ex-wife today?" Ralph said when I went into the kitchen for coffee.

"I said you could stay here, Ralph, I didn't say you could talk to me."

"Aww, come on," he wheedled in that falsely bright voice I hated, the one he used to use on me when he was trying to get back into my good graces. "You're my sister-in-law, and now my roomie again. Don't tell me that's not kinda beautiful, babe."

I put my coffee cup down hard on the kitchen island that separated us and leaned over, my face close to his.

"Listen to me, you pathetic little gnat's ass. You made our marriage miserable, and since we split up you have gone out of your way to make my life a living hell. If hate was an Olympic event, I'd get a gold medal every. single. day. Sandy said you could stay here and while I'm not thrilled about it, I respect him. You, I do not respect. So do not talk to me, do not get in my way, do not even breathe where I can hear you and do not call me babe. Ever."

My voice had dropped to a hiss. Ralph blinked like a cornered snapping turtle. At that moment, Sandy came into the kitchen, whistling and jingling the coins in his pocket like he always did.

"Morning, family!" he said, leaning down to kiss me.

"Morning, *babe*," I said, kissing him back and shooting one more meaningful look at Ralph. While Sandy happily poured himself and his little brother some coffee, I took a package of Fig Newtons out of the cupboard, sat down at the kitchen table, and proceeded to eat and read the paper. The brothers talked, Ralph having recovered some of his color, but I wrapped my protective cocoon around myself, the one I used whenever I needed to keep myself safe from anyone and anything since the day my mother walked out.

Whiskey Shots by the Light of the Moon

Sometimes I actually found it easy to forget that Ralph was living with me. I'd be working, lost in the mesmerizing feeling of clay taking shape in my fingers, or reading a book, or soaking in a bubble bath, and for awhile, I'd forget he was out there. Then he'd walk in the door or I'd turn around or look up and there was his stupid, arrogant head.

I tried to adapt, for Sandy's sake, I really did. I'd attempt conversation with him, or including him in whatever we were doing, but then he'd make some stupid crack or act like an ass or try to flirt with me, and I'd have to walk away before I went nuts and started burning stuff.

The worst part is it started to take a toll on my marriage to Sanford. I felt like he was turning a blind eye to how uncomfortable I was at having to share my space with my ex-husband. I began to see him less as a caring, giving man and more of a willfully ignorant beast for subjecting his wife to something so horrible.

"How many women would put up with this?" I ranted one night as we were getting ready for bed.

"What's wrong?" Sandy asked, with his usual mix of absentmindedness and good humor.

"Hey, Ari, where are the clean towels?" Ralph's voice, amplified and mushy from the crack between the door and the jamb, made me jump.

"THAT!" I mouthed to Sandy, pointing a furious finger at the door. He got up.

"I'll get him towels," he muttered, and went out, snapping the door closed behind him. I pulled on a ratty, oversized nightshirt, one that I knew was not only not sexy but actually kind of gross, and got into bed, rolling away from Sandy's side. A few minutes later, he came back in. He undressed silently and climbed into bed beside me, but didn't reach for me. We lay in silence for so long I thought he must have fallen asleep, until he spoke.

"You have been angry with me for weeks," he said. "Since the day I told Ralph he could move in here. But instead of just talking with me how you feel, you've reverted to the same passive-aggressive behavior I used to watch you use on Ralph."

I sat up and turned to stare at him.

"I can't believe what I'm hearing. You tell my ex-husband he can move in here, into MY home, and be in MY face every second of every day, and you expect me to just go about my life like nothing's wrong? He was abusive and horrible to me, Sandy, I'm sorry I can't just erase all of that from my memory! And I'm sorry you don't love me enough to try and protect me from him!"

I flung myself down and turned my back, tears stinging my eyes. After a moment, I felt his hand on my shoulder but I jerked away. He sighed, turned off the light, and laid back down. Eventually soft snores bubbled up from his side of the bed. How could he sleep when we'd just had a fight? He could at least have the consideration to pretend to still be upset.

I sat up and slid my feet into my slippers, grabbed my robe from the chair, and slipped quietly out of the bedroom and went into the kitchen. Light from the full moon had spilled everywhere, illuminating Roscoe, sound asleep in his bed next to the stove, the dish drainer full of clean plates and glasses, the art glass vase crammed with half-wilted wildflowers Sandy had brought home earlier in the week to surprise me, the morning newspaper strewn across the kitchen table, a stack of clean dishtowels on the hutch, near the drawer where they belonged, but not actually put away.

"My life is chaos," I whispered. I couldn't move, couldn't breathe, couldn't stop my whirling mind with both hands. Suddenly I gave a big gasp like a drowning woman who had just broken the surface of the water, then started to cry – hot, heavy, silent tears that slid down my face, fast and thick, soaking the neck of my nightshirt, splashing onto the floor, and making Roscoe get up and lean worriedly against my leg.

I went to the cabinet, reached up on the top shelf where we kept the whiskey we used for cooking, poured a half-inch into a juice glass, and knocked it back in one swallow. Standing in the dark kitchen, my breath coming in ragged, gasping half-hiccups, I realized how pitiful it was that my life was falling apart and all I could do was drink whiskey shots in my wet nightshirt. This wasn't going to fix anything. But as the warmth spread through me, I looked down at the bottle and shrugged. It also couldn't break it any more than it already was. I slammed down another shot, then put the bottle back, rinsed the glass and put it in the dish drainer.

"Come on, Rossie," I said, patting him on the head. He followed me into my studio where I wrapped myself in my quilt and sat down in the overstuffed arm chair. The dog climbed onto my lap, a long and arduous process given his bad hips and the fact that he weighed 65 pounds. I let him stay for a few minutes so he could feel he'd comforted me sufficiently before I gently shifted him back to the floor, which he greeted with a giant sigh. I sat back, wrapping my robe around me. The whiskey had taken away the hard, pinched feeling of despair that I'd been carrying around in my stomach since Ralph moved in. I let my eyes roam around my comforting studio. I could barely make out the outline of Brancusi's face on the wall, his features obscured by shadow. An anemic strand of moonlight struggled as far as the window screen but couldn't muster the strength to come inside. I stared out into the darkness, wondering what to do.

The next thing I knew, Sandy was gently shaking me awake. The room was bright and sunny and I had a little drool on my cheek.

"You okay?" Sandy said. "I was worried when I woke up and you weren't in bed."

"I'm fine," I answered, wiping my face with the back of my hand. "Sorry. I couldn't sleep so I got up and I guess I fell asleep here." My mouth tasted strange and it took me a moment to remember the two whiskey shots from the night before. I turned my head away slightly, hoping Sandy couldn't smell it. He sat down on the arm of the chair and took my hands in his.

"I'm sorry about last night," he said. "I was just frustrated and aggravated with you. I promised my mother when she was dying that I'd take care of the family, and I guess I was just pissed that you don't seem to understand or care that I'm only trying to do what I promised. But I also know it's not fair to you. Even if he wasn't your ex-husband, it's still hard to have someone else in the house. I will talk to him and see where he's at in the whole finding-his-own-place thing. Okay? I'm sorry. I love you."

I rested my forehead on his leg. "I'm sorry too," I said. "He's still your brother. I should have been more gracious about opening our home to him."

I could hear myself speaking the words, although I knew, in the privacy of my head, I didn't really mean it. But I was going to do my best to make sure Sandy never knew I didn't. I wasn't about to let Ralph ruin this marriage. He'd already ruined my first one.

Sidewalk Chalk and Roses

I was walking home from the afternoon shift at the library, wondering if there was anything else I could do while I was out so I could delay going home and having to see Ralph. It had been several months since he'd moved in and I still got a nasty little pinch in my gut when I walked in the door and saw him. It was as if when I wasn't home, I managed to forget he was living there. And when I came home and saw him, I got that sick, startled feeling. You know the one you get when you unexpectedly run into your ex somewhere? That one. Except I got it every time I came home. Even if he was out, I'd walk in and be reminded that he was still around, in my home, in my life. If it's starting to sound like I was feeling mighty sorry for myself, it's because I was.

In fact, I was indulging in copious amounts of self-pity as I rounded a corner and nearly stepped on a small girl of about six who was playing with sidewalk chalk. Nearby were about a half-dozen other young artists, all busily decorating the dull, gray San Francisco sidewalk with spongy soft pastel flowers, crookedly smiling faces, and those objets d'art that are crystal clear in the child's mind but a beautiful mystery to the rest of us.

"Hello," the girl closest to me said happily. "We're drawing!"

"I see that," I said, crouching down beside her and putting my nearly empty cup of coffee down carefully so I didn't mess up her work. "And you're doing a beautiful job. What are you drawing?"

"My house," she said, studying it. "It's a little bigger than this in real life, but I don't have enough sidewalk."

"That's all right," I reassured her. "Most art isn't the size it is in real life."

"Wanna draw with me?" she asked. She held up a bucket of fat, dusty pieces of chalk.

"Sure," I said. "Where's your mom, or your... babysitter?"

"She's in there." The little girl pointed in the window of a coffee shop. "This is our play group. Our moms sit in there and drink coffee and we draw out here."

"Oh I see," I said. I waved to the women in the window before sitting down cross-legged and reaching for a piece of chalk. "That sounds nice."

The girl shrugged.

"It's fun, but I think I'm going to be ready to move on from chalk soon."

I stifled a smile. "Is that right? What do you think you'd like to work in next? Paint?"

"Well, I have some paint at home, but it's all dried out. So is my Play Doh. I'm not sure but I think I might like to try colored pencils next."

"That's a good idea," I said. "Colored pencils are great. I use them myself sometimes."

"Are you an artist?" she asked me, scribbling hard to color in the roof of the house she was drawing.

"I am, yeah. I draw a little but mostly I'm a sculptor."

"Yeah, I know what you mean," she said. "Like I do with Play Doh."

While she chattered on about her various Play Doh creations, I pressed a piece of pink chalk against the sidewalk and pushed it forward, watching the broad, cottony line it left behind. Sometimes I wondered if I made art too difficult, if the times I was blocked were because I didn't just let it flow naturally. The chalk made a smooth right turn and soon I had layers of petals.

"Is that a flower?" my drawing companion asked.

"I think it is," I answered. "I think it's going to be a rose."

"That's my name!" she said, looking up at me with a delighted smile. "My name is Rose!"

"Well how do you like that?" I asked. "It's almost like I guessed, isn't it?"

"Finish the rose before I have to go!" she begged. "I'll get my mommy to take a picture of it with her phone."

"Okay," I said. "Finish your picture too, I know she'll like seeing that."

"What's your name?" Rose asked, adding a tree next to the house.

"Ariel."

"Like in the Little Mermaid."

"Yes. Just like that. Except I don't swim as good as she does."

Rose thought this was very funny. I finished the blossom of the flower and added a stem and leaves with her pale green chalk. I was just putting the chalk back in her little bucket when the door of the coffee shop sent the smell of roasted coffee and four women in jeans and sandals out onto the sidewalk.

"Mommy, look!" Rose called. "This is Ariel and she drew a rose for me!"

"Oh how lovely," her mother said. She smiled at me. I felt suddenly awkward, wondering if I looked like some kind of a creepy predator, hanging around with little kids I didn't know.

"I live a few blocks from here, I was just walking home from the library when I saw these great little artists and had to stop and admire their work. Your daughter persuaded me to join in."

The woman laughed.

"She's very persuasive. What did you draw, Rosie?"

"Our house. It's too little but Ariel said that art isn't the same size as real life."

"That's true," her mother agreed. "All right, let's get your stuff picked up. We have to go get Sawyer from swimming lessons and then it will be time to start dinner. Daddy will be home soon."

There was a flurry of activity as chalk went back into buckets and kids and moms divided themselves into the right groups and disappeared in different directions, back to their homes, their lives. I leaned back against the wall behind me, gazing at the drawings Rose and I had done. It didn't take a psychology degree to understand the gnawing feeling in my gut was a combination of my own long-forgotten longing to be a mother and the memory of myself at Rose's age, knowing with absolute, uncluttered, childlike certainty that I could be any kind of artist I wanted.

I pulled my knees up and rested my forehead on them, lost in thought until I heard a passerby drop a few coins into my coffee cup. Oh, very nice.

New York, New York, a Hell of a Town ...

It was strange enough to have gotten an e-mail from Lem, who had an account at my insistence but never used it because, as she put it, words flying through the air was creepy. But what was even stranger was the fact that it was about a juried art show in New York City that she thought I should enter. Strangest of all, I found myself considering it.

Except for a couple of small displays in the showcases at the library, I'd never actually had a real show. I'd thought about it, of course, imagining myself in a slinky black gown, hair piled glamorously on top of my head, glass of champagne twinkling in my hand as talked about my art in a deep, thoughtful way with my ardent admirers, my intellectual exterior broken only periodically by an abundant, sexy Julia Roberts laugh that I didn't actually have. Maybe being part of a show in New York would finally be my chance to shine. If I got in, which I knew was a pretty big if.

I was lining up the sculptures I'd collected from all over the house to see if any of them were good enough to enter when Ralph materialized in the doorway.

"Getting together with all your friends?"

I gritted my teeth.

"They all have stone heads, so I think they're actually your friends."

Ralph laughed a little too loudly, then went into the refrigerator, helped himself to a beer and disappeared into his room. I quelled the urge to pick up one of the biggest sculptures and hurl it after him.

I actually had amassed quite a few over the years. Some showed my early amateurish style, but others were really pretty good. I had gradually carved out a niche with asymmetrical heads and slitted eyes and noses. I couldn't miss the Brancusi influence when I looked at them, but they had my personal style, a look that was all my own. Early on, I had struggled to make mouths. They never looked right no matter what I did, so I always left the faces smooth between the nose and the chin, and eventually I realized I liked them mouthless. To me, they represented reticence, silence, holding back all that could be said but wasn't.

I went to the kitchen for some Fig Newtons, then came back and studied each sculpture, moving down the line, from figure to figure, my fingers trailing lightly over one head after the other as I remembered sculpting each of them, how I'd felt, where I'd been sitting, the wet clay cool in my hands. Sculpting wasn't something I'd set out to do, and I didn't study it in school – the college degree my father had insisted would make my life complete was in the broadly vague field of communication – but like Rose, I'd started out with Play Doh. On the days I was scheduled for artistic play, I'd experimented with rolling it, slicing it, pressing pieces together, and using my snub-nosed kid scissors to gouge out eyes and mouths. I remember the day I saw a commercial for that plastic press, where you could stuff the Play Doh in and squeeze down the handle and it would come out shaped like a long star or spaghetti strands or something. I was fascinated, not because I wanted one but because I couldn't believe any child would have such a complete lack of imagination as to use something like that to end up with a project that looked smooth and perfect and exactly the same every time.

My adult attempts at sculpture stood before me now, like a military roll call, each one waiting to be deemed worthy to enter into the show in New York. One by one, I passed over them. None of them were right. None of them represented what I wanted to say right now. I carried them all over and put them on the windowsill and the small shelf on the wall, then dropped a Mozart CD onto the stereo, sat down and unwrapped a fresh lump of clay. I picked it up, my hands cupped around it, and held it close to me for a long moment, my eyes closed, sending the warmth of my body into the coldness of the clay, infusing it with my spirit, willing it to become art and beauty. It was my ritual, always had been, before starting a new piece.

Unfortunately, this one was just a nasty little clay bastard. I spent an hour wrestling with it, and nothing was coming. Usually a new piece of clay started to find its own shape as I worked, but this one wanted no part of me. I reached for one of my millions of sketchbooks where I often sketched ideas for sculptures, and thumbed through it. Nothing.

"Hey." Sanford's voice in the doorway made me jump.

"Hey," I said. He came in and kissed me on top of the head.

"What are you working on?"

"A pile of shit that hates me."

"Nice. That will look good on the nameplate underneath."

I groaned.

"I was doing fine until Lem sent me an email about a juried show in New York and I think I might want to enter. Now I can't come up with anything decent."

"New York?"

"Yeah." I slapped the clay with the heel of my hand.

"We live in San Francisco."

"Yeah? So? I'm not saying we should move to New York, I'm just thinking of entering a show there."

"Okay, sure, why not?"

"It doesn't matter anyway, I can't seem to come up with anything that I wouldn't be mortified to have someone else see."

"What? You're nuts. Look at these – these are great." He went over to the busts I'd lined up.

"No, they're horrible. That's why I put them there."

"They do look a little like they're facing a firing squad," he observed. "Well, if you're not happy with them, make something else."

"Thanks, Captain Obvious. That's what I'm doing but it's not working."

He came up behind me and rubbed my shoulders.

"Come on," he said. "You need to take a break. Why don't we go out and get some dinner? I don't feel like cooking."

"Okay," I said. "The more I work the more aggravated I get."

"Is it okay with you if I ask Ralph to go with us? I won't if you don't want me to."

"I can hardly say we're going out and he can't come," I said. "So what's the difference? I'll make us a cocktail before we go."

Sandy gave me an odd look and went out. I could hear him talking to Ralph in the next room. I wrapped the clay in plastic and went to wash my hands. Then I rummaged around in the cupboard and pulled out a bottle of wine someone had given us once for a gift. It was a sweet red spiced wine, my favorite. I was pouring it into juice glasses when Sandy came in.

"What's the occasion?" he asked. "You're not usually much of a drinker."

"Eh, I just felt like it," I said. "You don't mind?"

"Nope," he said, taking a glass and handing one to Ralph as he walked in the door.

"A toast," Sandy said. "To … uh… to Ariel's art being chosen for the show in New York!"

"What show?" Ralph asked.

"Nothing," I said hurriedly. "I don't even know if I'm entering. It's nothing."

"Oh, well, cheers anyway," Ralph said, taking a big swallow of wine. "Wow, what is this crap? It's nasty."

"Come on," Sandy said. "Let's get out of here or the restaurant will be a madhouse. I'll bring the car around. I had to park it all the way down the block."

"I'll walk with you," Ralph said, putting his glass down. I gathered up the wine glasses as they headed out. The door closed behind them and I looked down at the glasses, each with that beautiful wine shimmering in the bottom. It wasn't nasty. I loved it. I drained my glass and Sandy's, then poured the rest of Ralph's down the sink. It didn't matter how much I loved it, I wasn't putting my mouth anywhere near where his had been.

Feeling slightly giddy from the wine, I put my shoes on and grabbed my jacket just as the car pulled up.

Lem's Surprise

I don't know what I expected Lem to say when I picked up the phone, but telling me she was pregnant wasn't on the list of possibilities.

"You're what?"

"I'm going to have a baby," she said. I could hear the smile in her voice.

"What? Since when? When did this happen? How did this happen?"

"Well, when a man and a woman love each other…"

"Who is the man you love?" I interrupted.

"River," she said, dreamily. "He has big, gentle hands and long hair. Such an earthy spirit."

"And he knocked you up? Lem! What were you thinking?"

"He is my soul mate," she said.

"Where is he now?" I demanded.

"Out in the garden, I think. I'll look." There was a pause and I knew exactly what she was doing. She had crossed the room and moved the curtains aside and she was looking down into the garden where he may well have been at one point, but now I'd have bet anything he was…

"Gone," Lem said. "He's gone. He must have gone out for more mulch."

Yeah, that's what we'll say. Mulch.

"Lem," I said gently. "I think we need to talk. Why don't I come over?"

"You are always welcome here," she said serenely. "But if you're coming over because you are worried about me, it's not necessary. I'm fine."

"I'm still coming over," I said. "I'll be there in 30 minutes."

When I pulled up outside of Lem's complex, I could see that new work had been done in the garden, but there was still no gardener in sight. I walked around the building to be sure, but there was no one. There wasn't even evidence that anyone was still working and had just run out for supplies. Everything was tidy. I pushed the bell for her apartment and, as usual, the door buzzed without her asking who it was. No wonder the gardener found it so easy to come up.

I hugged her when I got inside. She was smiling, soft and floaty as always.

"Lem, tell me what happened," I said, taking her hand as I sat down beside her.

"I told you already. His name is River, and he is the gardener here," she said. "Actually, he said he's a landscape artist."

"Of course he is," I said. "But how did you... hook up?"

"He would always smile at me when I passed, and you know that smiles are bridges we build between our souls," she said. "So one day he took my hand and told me that in another life, we had been lovers."

"So you decided to be lovers in this life too."

She pulled her hand away.

"I am sensing judgment from you."

"No no, honey, I'm not judging you, I'm just concerned about you. Does River know you're pregnant?"

"Of course," she said. "I told him the moment it happened. I felt our life forces connect inside me."

"And that didn't freak him out?"

"Oh no," she said. "He cried and said it was all so beautiful."

"When was this?"

"What does time matter when two souls are-"

"Lem! When did it happen? Think. It's important."

She hemmed and hawed and thumbed through her Dream Book

and her Life Log and her watercolor finger paintings and finally decided it had been about three weeks ago.

"But you can't know you're pregnant yet," I said. "It hasn't been long enough."

"I do know," she said gently.

I shook my head."Even a pregnancy test wouldn't tell you yet," I said. "It's too early."

She looked at me levelly.

"Ariel, how long have we known each other?"

"I don't know. A long time."

"And do you not yet know me well enough to be sure that I know what's going on in my own body?"

I was never even sure Lem knew what year it was half the time, but I didn't say so.

"You know I don't believe in Western medicine, but let's go to the store and get a test," she said. "I'll show you."

We piled into my car and headed to the drug store a couple of miles away. Twenty minutes later, we were back at Lem's apartment. I sat on the couch and waited while she peed on the stick. She came out of the bathroom carrying it like a torch. She sat down beside me and we watched the little window, waiting. Slowly, gradually, both lines turned dark purple.

"Son of a ..." My voice dropped to a creaking whisper as I looked up at Lem's smiling face. "You're pregnant."

When Pizza, Clay and Brancusi Collide

When I got home, there was a note from Sandy that he and Ralph had gone out to shoot some pool and would bring a pizza back later for dinner. I was glad for the reprieve as I needed to mull over what had just happened with Lem. I took Roscoe, who expressed no interest whatsoever in going, for a walk and when we came back in, I fed him, then poured myself a big glass of wine and went into my studio. I turned on the stereo and sat down on my stool. I rested my chin in my hand and stared unseeingly at the smooth, featureless blob of clay on top of the armature. Lem was going to have a baby. It didn't seem possible. In some ways, Lem still was a baby, how was she going to cope? And this River person… let's just say I'd have been amazed if he wasn't already high-tailing it for Mexico, love beads and hemp curtains flapping wildly in the back of his van as he picked up speed.

I took a long sip of wine and looked up at Brancusi. With a sigh, I put the glass down and unwrapped the clay. It felt different in my hands this time – a bit firmer, yet somehow easier to mold. I pushed and pulled, kneaded and prodded and rolled. There was a shape there, something wanting to come out. I couldn't see it yet, but I could finally sense that it was there. Oddly, it wasn't asymmetrical as usual, but round. I reached for my reading glasses, took another drink of wine, and bent over the clay, eager now.

"Ari?"

Sandy's voice in the doorway startled me. I looked up, disoriented, pushing a piece of hair back from my face.

"Hi babe, I didn't hear you come in."

He crossed the room and kissed me. "That's why I didn't want to scare you," he said. "How's it going? Better?"

"I think so," I said. He didn't ask anything else as he knew I don't like to talk about my work when it's in the early stages for fear of chasing away the Muse. Mine is the jealous type.

"So," I said, straightening and stretching my back. "Lem is pregnant."

"Wow, really?"

"Yeah, I didn't believe it but we took a test this afternoon and she definitely is."

"Who's the lucky daddy?"

"The gardener at her apartment complex," I said. "If you can believe that."

Sandy shrugged.

"Why not? Gardeners have needs too."

"Very funny. I'm worried about her. I didn't even see this guy around today, or anything that would make me believe he's coming back."

"What does Lem say?"

"Oh, you know Lem. She's convinced he's her soul mate and that he just ran out for mulch and he'll be right back."

"Maybe she's right. I hope she is."

"I hope so too, but Lem isn't really the best judge of character. Half the time I'm not even sure Lem knows where she is."

Sandy smiled.

"Yes, she's a little spacey, but I think we maybe have to give her the benefit of the doubt on this one."

"Why?"

"First of all, why not? And second of all, it's really none of our business. She may seem like a ditzy 13-year-old, but she's a grown woman. She knows what she's doing."

"You're probably the only one who has ever accused her of that."

There was a pause before Sandy said "You're not jealous, are you?"

"No," I said. "I'm perfectly comfortable with our decision not to have children. I don't want to screw up a kid like my mother did with me."

"You're far from screwed up," he said, folding me into his arms. "But I thought maybe seeing Lem pregnant might make you re-think the decision."

I turned slightly in his arms to look up at his face.

"Why? Have you decided you want children now?"

"Nah." He kissed me on top of the head. "I don't want to share you."

I laughed.

"Did you bring home pizza like you promised? I'm starving."

"Yes, I put it in the oven to warm it up. Ralph met some friends of his at the bar so he stayed out with them. It's just you and me tonight."

"Wow, I almost forgot what that's like."

He gave me his naughty-boy grin.

"Let's not waste it."

It's a Sign...

I was bent over my work table, trying to smooth out an edge when my cell phone rang. I always keep it on the table next to me so I don't have to dig it out of my pocket when my hands are full of clay. It was Lem. Using one knuckle, I pushed the button to answer and another button to put it on speaker phone.

"Hey Lem," I said.

"Hey Ariel."

There was a bit of silence.

"What's up?" I asked. Lem often needed prompting to remember why she called.

"I need to go shopping," she said.

"Shopping for what? You hate shopping."

"I hate shopping at the mall and other big, shiny stores that are an affront to the environment and feed the insatiable beast of consumerism," she corrected me. "Also fluorescent lights are bad for my psyche. But I want to go to a place I've heard about, a ways out in the country."

"What kind of a place?" I wasn't keen on going out just when I thought my piece might be starting to take shape, but I had agreed long ago to drive Lem anyplace she needed to go. She'd voluntarily surrendered her driver's license after swerving to avoid running over a squirrel and instead hitting a telephone pole, sending it crashing down in a perfectly straight line on top of five parked cars.

"It's a place that sells baby clothes made from natural fibers, organic bath products, that kind of stuff," she said. "I need to get a few things."

"River can't drive you?"

"He's working," she said.

"Oh, really? At your complex? I'd love to meet him when I come pick you up."

"Not here," she said. "He's done with the garden here until the season changes again. He's working somewhere else."

"Mmm," I said. "Okay, so when do you want to go?"

"Right now."

Naturally.

"Okay, let me wash up and I'll come get you." Half an hour later, I pulled up in front of her building to find her outside, sitting on the ground, her legs stretched in front of her, her skirt spread out on the grass. When she saw me, she got up and floated to the car. I hugged her when she sat down.

"What are you doing outside?" I asked.

"My little butterfly wanted some sunshine and fresh air," she said, patting her tummy.

"Wouldn't it be a chrysalis?" I asked, pulling away from the curb. Lem made a face.

"I don't like to think of it like that," she said. "I feel as though I have a tiny butterfly inside me, waiting to burst into full color, new life, taking wing..." She suddenly looked as though she might cry.

"That's beautiful, honey," I said soothingly. "I think it is a butterfly, a beautiful butterfly like her mommy."

"It might be a boy," Lem said, sniffling delicately. I laughed. I couldn't help it.

"Yes, it might be," I said. I wanted to ask her more about River, I wanted to tell her I was worried about her, but she seemed even more fragile than usual today. Instead, I put on the 60s station and we rocked out to some hippie tunes, singing along at the top of our lungs.

"Here it is," Lem said suddenly, turning down the radio and pointing.

"Where?"

"On the other side of these trees," she said. "Turn left into the drive right after the trees."

I pulled in and stopped, then just sat there, gawking. It was a farm – a giant spread of a farm – with overgrown vegetable and flower gardens, and herbs in pots scattered everywhere. Tiny children, most of them naked, were running and shrieking across what could be described as a lawn, although it seemed to be covered with everything except grass. There was an enormous and dilapidated old barn, and a huge, ramshackle house that had vines, I swear to God, growing from the inside out. There were giant, strange sculptures of metal and stone scattered about, and at least six different kinds of ancient, gnarled trees. I'd driven into a Roald Dahl novel.

"Isn't it beautiful?" Lem said happily.

"It's... beautiful," I echoed. A child clad only in Spiderman underwear suddenly dropped out of one of the trees close to the car, and I jumped and shrieked.

"Come on," Lem said. "I want to meet Cora!"

"Cora?" I asked, stepping out of the car.

"She's the woman who runs the business. She lives here with her kids," Lem explained. A child of about six ran past, pushing two squealing toddlers in a wheelbarrow. "These are her kids," she added unnecessarily.

"How did you find this place?"

"On the Web," Lem said importantly.

"Oh, did you now? You said the web was creepy."

"It is creepy. But I wanted to find a place where I could buy organic, natural, handmade things for my butterfly, and this came up."

As we approached the house, I could see a hand-painted wooden sign over the doorway that said "The Enchanted Elf." A cat with one ear dozed on a decrepit rocking chair near the door, and a cracked clay pot with about two hundred different kinds of flowers jammed together stood on the other side. Lem tapped on the door and a woman's voice called out "You kids quit that racket out there! Mama's working!"

Lem laughed.

"Sorry, Mama, but we're customers!" she called. A tiny woman with a giant cloud of red hair materialized in the doorway.

"Oh my goodness, I'm so sorry! Come on in. Those kids have been murder today, running in and out constantly, slamming the door and I don't know what all."

We stepped inside.

"I'm Lem, and this is my friend Ariel," Lem said. "I found you on the Web."

"I'm Cora," the woman said. "Isn't that nice? I'm glad you're here. Are you looking for anything in particular? My shop is back this way."

We followed her through an oddly beautiful, cluttered, warm home that smelled faintly of cooking and glue and apple juice and patchouli.

"Well, I'm having a baby and I wanted to get a few things," Lem said. Cora gave her an odd look.

"You're having a baby? You don't look like it."

"She's just barely pregnant, but she likes to plan ahead," I said.

"Plan ahead," Lem echoed absently, gazing around the shop in wonder. She was right – it was magnificent. Jutting off the back of the house, the entire shop had once been a greenhouse but was now filled with shelves and tables overflowing with beautiful baby clothes, blankets and soft toys, all clearly handmade. But the most breathtaking part was the ceiling. It was hung with thousands of delicate glass butterflies, in a million colors, hanging at varying heights, catching the light and swaying gently. Lem grabbed my hand.

"Ari," she whispered. "Butterflies! It's a sign!"

Her face looked positively angelic as she gazed upward, her eyes wide as a child's. I felt tears catch in my throat and I squeezed her hand.

"Yes, my love, it's a sign."

A Drink… to Motherhood

As I was taking Roscoe for a walk later, I wondered if I actually was jealous of Lem. When I was growing up, I'd dreamed of being a mother. I'd get one of my dolls dressed before my parents and I left the house for our Saturday errands, making sure she had on the proper shoes and a bonnet to keep her from getting chilly. At the stores I'd put her in the child seat of the shopping cart and pretend I was buying groceries for my own family. My favorite trips were those to home improvement stores, where I'd walk among the shiny new sinks and faucets and light fixtures, mentally putting them in my imagined home and quietly telling my doll how we were going to decorate her room.

But reality didn't have that kind of a future in mind for me. Ralph and I had never discussed children, mostly because we both knew how babies are made and that wasn't happening. But once I was with Sandy, who I knew would be a great father, I had to examine my own heart and decide if I thought I could be a mother. I love children and at some level I did want to do it, but on a bigger and much deeper level, I was scared to death that I'd end up causing hurt and damage to my child, as my mother had done to me. What if I didn't know how to love like a mother should? I could never walk out the door and disappear on my child, but what if I shut myself off emotionally? Wasn't that kind of abandonment almost worse?

In the end, I debated it for so long that I entered my 40s and knew that if nature hadn't already made the decision for me, she would soon. But now, watching Lem's happiness over her impending motherhood pinched at my insides more than I wanted to admit. I hung Roscoe's leash on its hook by the back door, then followed him into the kitchen. He went straight for his food bowl, I went straight for the cabinet where I'd stashed a new bottle of whiskey, far behind the boxes of rice and pasta we never used. I did two fast shots, then mixed another with some soda and ice before putting the bottle back and covering it up. I carried the drink into my studio and unwrapped the lump of clay. I stared at it for a long time, mesmerized, wondering, visualizing. When I realized my glass was empty, I put it into the desk drawer, stuffed a piece of gum in my mouth so I didn't smell like booze, and picked up a tiny sculpting knife. An hour later, all I had was a ball of clay covered in frustrated little gouge marks. I smoothed them back out before wrapping it in plastic and, avoiding Brancusi's eyes, shut off the light and walked out.

Who's He Calling Grandma?

As the days stretched into weeks, I tried to adjust to having Ralph living with us. I figured it would be easier to try and get myself used to it, instead of watching the calendar and wondering how much longer it could possibly last. Those kinds of thoughts only made me angry.

One gorgeous morning, the kind that I immediately put at the top of my list of Reasons Why I Never Want to Live Anywhere Except San Francisco, Roscoe and I had gone out for a long, early walk. On the way back, I stopped for coffee and a Chronicle. I came in just as Sandy was leaving for the gallery.

"Hi and bye," he said, kissing me. "I didn't even hear you get up."

"I couldn't sleep, so Rossie and I decided we could use a long walk."

Sandy rubbed the dog affectionately on the head.

"Your new medicine is making you feel better, isn't it, Ros? That coffee smells great," he said. "Better than the green tea I had."

"Yours is healthier," I said. "I'm going to grab a shower and then I want to get a little work done on a couple of pieces before I have to head over to the library."

"You're working this afternoon?"

"Filling in. One of the college students is out sick so I told them I'd do it. I'll be home by 6."

Our domestic meeting finished, Sandy left for work. As soon as he was gone, I fed Roscoe, then spread the Chronicle out on the kitchen table, rifling through the sections until I found the classifieds. I folded it open to the "help wanted" section, which I carried into the living room and put in the middle of the sofa cushion where Ralph couldn't miss it when he finally dragged his butt out of bed. I knew he'd see it – that's where he sat all day and played on his laptop or watched TV while Sandy and I worked. I was being completely passive-aggressive, I knew, but every time I tried to say anything to Ralph about maybe getting another job and moving the hell out of my house, he turned it into a huge fight, and Sandy would get upset and try to mediate, which just made me angrier. He should take my side, for crying out loud, I'm his wife. But Sandy continued to insist we were all a family and that families love each other, and Ralph continued being a nasty little pinhead, so passive-aggressive it would have to be.

An hour later, I was in my studio working when Ralph shuffled into the kitchen. I could hear the clunk of the coffee pot as he helped himself, then he shuffled into the living room. I smiled when the shuffling stopped.

"Very funny!" I heard him yell from the living room. "Nobody finds jobs in the classifieds anymore, GRANDMA."

I got up and closed the door, then went back to work. I didn't want to hear him watching The View, or whatever his current, incongruous daytime TV addiction was. At lunchtime, I went into the kitchen and grabbed a yogurt, a package of Fig Newtons and the rest of the newspaper, then went back into my studio. There was a time when I would have eaten lunch and read the paper at the kitchen table, but I didn't want to see or talk to Ralph until I absolutely had to. I hated having him around, I hated that I felt like a prisoner in my own house. I swallowed my rising anger and washed it down with three Fig Newtons before getting back to work, blocking all thoughts of Ralph by focusing on my art.

I ended up leaving the library a little early as things were quiet, and the full-time staffer I was working with offered to lock up. It was fine with me – I was exhausted. Several nights of fitful sleep were starting to catch up with me. When I got home, I took Roscoe for a short walk, and when I came back in, started to wonder what was keeping Sandy. I had just dumped kibble into the dog's dish when I got a text saying he had been held up a bit by a particularly chatty patron and would be home in an hour. I wasn't sure I was going to be able to keep my eyes open that long. I could hear Ralph on the phone in his room, so I poured myself a whiskey and soda, stashed the bottle again, and went into my studio to look at the pieces I'd been working on that morning. Whenever I was blocked on one piece, it usually helped to put it aside for awhile and work on something else. These looked pretty good and I decided to go ahead and let two of them start drying. The other one still needed something, I just didn't know what.

I wrapped it back up, then pushed the stool in and sat down on the floor, leaning back against the wall. I looked around the room, with all of its familiar objects, and up at Brancusi who was, as usual, regarding me with a serious expression. I used to tell myself he was thinking about how much he'd like to sculpt me. Lately I figured he was just finding me pathetic. And as I drained the whiskey and soda and went back into the kitchen to wash and dry the glass, then into the bathroom to brush my teeth before Sandy came home, I realized he'd be right.

Ralph's Surprise

I shifted the heavy bag of clay to my other hand and fumbled in my bag for the key, which had naturally gone straight to the bottom. When my fingers finally found it, I pulled it out triumphantly, only to drop it. It hit my foot, bounced into a beautiful arc, sailed off the porch and landed in the bushes.

"Son… of … a… BITCH!" I shrieked. I set the bag down, stomped down the steps and crawled into the bushes, getting my hair stuck in twigs that heartlessly scratched my face and poked into my ear.

"I planted you, you stupid bush, I water you. You watch yourself or you'll be mulch." I finally found the key, crawled out, got my bag and let myself into the house. Dropping everything onto the table, I pushed my hair back out of my face, wincing as my hand brushed a scratch on my cheek. I went into the bathroom to inspect the damage. I had a nice long scratch on the left side of my face, a smaller one above my eye, and assorted leaves stuck in my hair. I looked like a deranged Mother Nature. I plucked out the leaves, ran a brush through my hair, then washed my hands and dabbed a little antiseptic on my wounds.

Roscoe wandered into the bathroom and seemed surprised to see me.

"Hello, Rossie, you old dog. Where were you when Mommy needed help getting her key out of the bushes?" He sat down on the floor and thumped his tail agreeably.

"Yeah, you talk big," I said. "We both know you'd never have gone under that bush. Come on, Mommy needs a drink."

I went into the kitchen and pulled out my secret bottle of whiskey. I'd discovered that if I mixed it with orange juice, it wouldn't appear to anyone else that I was drinking anything other than juice. Not that I was really hiding my drinking from Sandy, I just didn't want him to worry. Glancing down at the bottle, I saw that it was almost half gone and I'd only had it a week. Maybe I should slow down a bit. It helped so much, though. It was almost medicinal, the way it took the edge off, made Lem's pregnancy sting a little less, made the invasion of my ex-husband into my home a bit easier to take. The only thing it couldn't do was change the way I felt about Ralph. I'd stopped complaining about him to Sandy, and I could tell he was happier, satisfied that I'd gotten over it. The booze cast a soft, gauzy layer between me and my life so I could function without acting like a total bitch.

I mixed a second drink, hid the bottle again, then retreated into my studio with my new bag of clay. I put on the stereo, sat down and unwrapped the clay. I pushed and rolled and worked, looking for the inspiration that usually started to flow when my hands touched the clay. Nothing. I got up and pulled out one of my art books, hoping for a flash of something. Anything. Soon I was so absorbed in my reading that I jumped when I heard the back door open. I quickly shoved my empty glass under my sculpting table and blocked it with my foot.

"In here!" I called. Sandy appeared in the doorway, Ralph right behind him.

"Hi babe," Sandy said.

"Hello, my love," I answered, turning my face up for his kiss.

"Hi babe!" Ralph said from the doorway.

"Hello, Gnat's Ass," I said, then laughed. Ralph laughed like it was the funniest thing he'd ever heard. After looking at us both like we had officially lost our minds, Sandy laughed too.

"Are you at a stopping place?" Sandy asked. "Ralph wants to take us out to dinner. He said he has some big news to share with us. What happened to your face?"

I wrapped the clay and dropped my tools back into the flowerpot.

"Oh, I dropped my key into the bush and the bush decided to fight back. So what's your big news, Ralphie Boy?"

"I'm not telling until we are out where we can properly celebrate," he said. "You're still not the most patient person on the planet, are you?"

"No," I said. "Tell me now. Tell me noooooooooooow." I was feeling a bit giggly and Sandy gave me a strange look.

"I'm kidding," I said. "I can wait. I'm totally so patient in my old age. I'll just go wash my hands."

An hour later, when we were seated at a cute bistro downtown, Ralph cleared his throat theatrically and raised his wine glass.

"I am getting married," he said grandly, then looked at us expectantly. Sandy and I stared at him.

"What?" Sandy finally said.

"I'm getting married again!" Ralph repeated. We both just kept staring at him. "Hey, I'm no etiquette expert, but I think this is where you're supposed to congratulate me."

"Congratulations," I said. "I think we're just…"

"Surprised," Sandy finished. "I didn't even know you were seeing anyone. You never mentioned going on dates or anything."

"I met her online," Ralph said. "On a dating site. We've been talking for awhile, and I just knew she was the one. You know how it is when you just know?"

Sandy smiled.

"Yeah, I know that feeling well." He took my hand and squeezed it. Ralph rolled his eyes.

"Yeah, well, anyway, I asked her to marry me and she said yes."

"That's great," I said, lifting my own glass. "I'm really happy for you."

"Thanks, Ariel," he said, looking almost sincere. "I appreciate that."

I took a long pull on my wine while Sandy grilled him for details. Where did she live? What was her name? When were we going to meet her? When was the wedding? Her name was Ellen, she lived in Chicago, they hadn't set a wedding date yet and oh look, she was walking in the door of the bistro right that moment.

"What?" Sandy said. "That's her?" He gestured toward a leggy blonde who had just walked in. I could see a cab pulling away from the curb.

"I told her to meet me here." Ralph laughed, a deep, joyous sound I'd never heard from him. "I wanted it to be a surprise."

"You've never met her in person before either!" Sandy hissed as Ellen picked her way through the crowded bistro.

"We've talked on the phone, and on Skype," Ralph said. "I thought it would be fun for us all to meet at once."

Fun, yeah. Sure. I was half in the bag from the two whiskey drinks I'd had before they'd even come home, now I was about to be thrown into what could potentially be the most awkward situation of my life, watching my ex-husband and his new e-mail order bride getting to know each other while I held hands with his brother, who was now my husband. My head hurt. I poured another glass of wine as Ralph stood up and hugged the blonde. They hugged for a long time, not even noticing anyone else. When Ralph finally pulled away, I could see there were tears in his eyes.

"I never thought this day would come," he said. "I'm sorry I didn't pick you up at the airport but I wanted it to be just like this. You, here with me and my family, in our usual hangout... it feels like you stepped out of my dreams and into my life. It's perfect."

If there was one thing Ralph appreciated, it was perfection. I studied her surreptitiously. She looked normal enough.

"This is my brother, Sandy, and his wife, Ariel," he introduced us. She shook Sandy's hand first, then mine. Her nails were flawlessly manicured, her handshake that limp, cool variety that some women seem to think is feminine.

"It's nice to meet you both," she said.

"We're happy to meet you too, Ellen," Sandy said politely. "You'll have to excuse us, we didn't even know you existed until about four minutes ago."

"Ralph, did you keep me a secret?" She smiled at him as she sat down.

"I wanted it to be a surprise," he said, beaming at her. I'd never seen him look so happy.

"We're definitely surprised," Sandy said. "Aren't we, babe?"

I realized I hadn't yet spoken.

"Yes," I said. "Surprised and really happy for both of you."

After we'd ordered, Ralph poured more wine for all of us.

"A toast," he said. "To new beginnings and happy endings."

"Hear, hear!" Sandy said. I forced a smile and clinked glasses with the rest of them. I couldn't define what was bothering me. I wasn't jealous – God knows if this woman was willing to take Ralph out of my life I'd happily pay her. It wasn't that I didn't want to see Ralph happy, because I did. There was no rational explanation for the fact that something in this whole thing made me feel like I'd been kicked in the ribs. But there wasn't a chance in hell I was going to let it show. I poured myself a little more wine and gave Ellen a bright smile.

"So Ellen, what do you do?"

"I'm a dancer," she said.

"A dancer, wow," I said. "Like, exotic?"

"Ariel!" Ralph looked irritated, but Ellen laughed.

"It's okay, I get that question a lot. No, I'm actually with the Chicago Ballet. The tips aren't as good, though." Now everyone laughed, including Ralph.

"Ballet, that's awesome," I said. The wine was starting to get to me. I hoped I wasn't slurring my words.

"I've never done anything else," she said. "It's my passion. Ralph tells me you're an artist."

"We both are," I said, gesturing to Sandy. My lips and tongue were definitely wanting to slur, so I made myself speak carefully. "I'm a sculptor and he's a painter."

"That's wonderful," she said. "I'd love to see some of your work. Both of you."

"Oh you will," Ralph said. "Especially Ariel's – she has stuff scattered everywhere. I've never seen a messier artist."

I bit back a sharp answer and fortunately at that moment the food arrived. My head was spinning a bit and I quickly ate some bread, hoping to slow the wine's trip through my system. I had just stuffed a third piece into my mouth when I noticed Ellen was watching me. I tried to smile and some crumbs fell out of my mouth and onto my plate. Lovely. I swallowed the bread with some water and wiped my mouth on my napkin. I picked up my fork and cut into the ravioli.

"How is it?" Sandy asked. "Good?"

"Yes," I said. "Very." Ralph ordered another bottle of wine from a passing waiter, and before I knew it, my glass was brimming again. Oh what the hell. It's not like anyone was going to notice. Even Sandy seemed quite taken with Miss Ballerina. Miss Twinkletoes. Twinkletoes McTutu. I gave a little snorting laugh, and everyone looked at me.

"That's true," I said, hoping it fit with whatever someone else had just said. "So funny."

Ralph gave me a look and turned his attention back to Ellen. Sandy put his arm around me and whispered "Are you all right?" into my ear. "I'm fine," I whispered back. "Just a little tired and I think the wine is starting to get to me."

"You can switch to water," he said. "No one will think it's rude."

"I will after this glass," I said.

But I didn't. As the evening wore on, the mood became more and more festive as the wine flowed freely. I knew I was drunk, but I didn't realize how drunk until I stood up to go to the ladies' room. I felt the room move with me, and the last thing I remember was hitting the floor.

The Harsh Light of Reality

When I awoke the next morning, my mouth full of cotton, my head pounding, stomach churning, I reached for Sandy only to find the bed empty. I tried to sit up but my head throbbed so much I had to lay back down. I pulled the pillow over my head with a groan.

A moment later I heard the bedroom door open and felt the bed dip slightly.

"Babe?" I said, not moving the pillow.

"I'm here," I heard Sandy say. "How are you feeling?"

"Like I'm dead. Or wish I was."

I didn't want to sit up. I didn't want to face Sandy or anyone ever again.

"Come on out," he said. "I brought you coffee and aspirin."

I gingerly pulled the pillow off my face and slowly sat up, leaning back against the headboard. I swallowed the aspirin with a sip of coffee and grimaced. Sandy glanced at me, then looked down at his hands. He didn't speak.

"I think I drank too much last night," I said finally.

"I think you did," he said. "And I think we need to talk."

I closed my eyes.

"I know I shouldn't have had so much, but don't worry. I'm never drinking again."

"Everyone says that when they're hung over, but Ari, this is more than just last night. You've been drinking a lot lately, and I'm worried about you."

"I don't drink that much," I said, aware that I was lying, and lying poorly. Sandy knew too.

"Ariel, please listen to me," he said. "I found your stash of whiskey when I was looking for the honey the other day, and the bottle I didn't even know was there is nearly empty. I had been wondering why all our juice glasses were slowly disappearing, so I went looking for them and I found one under the couch, one under your sculpting table and one in a drawer in your art room. Ari... look at me. If you're hiding your drinking from me, I think we have a problem."

I couldn't meet his eyes. I stared down into my coffee cup, willing away the headache, the memories, the hurt.

"Ariel," he said softly, taking my hand. "You are the love of my life. I will do anything to help you."

I wanted to cry but I couldn't. I put my cup on the nightstand and shook my head. I opened my mouth but no words came out. I shook my head again. Sandy came around to my side of the bed and gathered me into his arms.

"What is it, my love?" he whispered into my hair. "Talk to me."

I couldn't even answer him. Finally he kissed me on top of my head.

"Try to sleep for awhile," he said. "I'll come back in a bit with some food."

"Okay," I said quietly. He pulled the door closed behind him as he left, and I rolled onto my side and stared at the curtain, darkened by the blind. How could I tell him that having Ralph here was messing with me to the point that I didn't know how to handle it? The last time I'd tried to talk to him about it, we'd had a huge fight. And anyway, I assumed Ralph would be moving out soon now that he was getting married again. I thought back to the night before. How could Ralph just waltz back into my life, ruin it, then waltz back out with his new love like nothing ever hap-pened? I wanted so much to have a good, long cry but there was nothing left. I was dried out, empty. Closing my eyes, I slept.

Lem Dyes Her Hair Blue, Makes Sense Again

"You're going to dye your ears blue if you don't stop moving around," I said crossly, holding the bottle of "Hippie Hippie Hooray Organic Funky Hair Hue" poised over Lem's head.

"It washes off," she said serenely. "It's fine."

"It does not wash off, it's permanent color."

"Nothing is permanent."

I can't argue with her with she gets all philosophical like that, so I just dabbed the last of the dye onto her head, cleaned off her skin with a washcloth, and set the timer on the stove. The bottle said the dye would wash out in 10-12 shampoos, so whatever. Lem made us tea and we sat down at the kitchen table.

"So, how is Rudy?"

"Ralph."

"Yes. Is he behaving himself?"

"I guess," I said. "He's not around as much lately. He's engaged."

"Oh wow," she said. "I didn't know that."

"None of us did until the other night," I said. "He had her fly in from Chicago to surprise us."

"I sense that he wanted to surprise you," Lem said, licking her thumb and rubbing a bit of blue dye off the table top.

"Yes, I think he did. He succeeded too. I had no idea he was even seeing anyone, and all of a sudden this leggy blonde thing folded herself through the doorway and bang, he's engaged."

"What's she like?"

I shrugged.

"She's okay," I said. "She was nice enough. Too good for Ralph, of course."

"So how long until the wedding? Or are they moving in together sooner?"

"I don't know. She went back to Chicago a couple of days ago. I haven't seen Ralph much since then so I haven't asked him. It might have come up that night but -" I hesitated. I was still embarrassed about how drunk I'd been and didn't want to think about it, let alone admit it to Lem.

She got up to pour more tea.

"I think this situation overall is healthy for you."

"Healthy? Are you nuts?"

She smiled absently, rearranging the lemon slices she'd put out on a tiny plate.

"I think you need closure with Rex, and this will give it to you."

"Ralph."

"Yes. You went from a bad marriage into a good one, but unlike most people, you married your brother-in-law. So now you must find a way to make peace with your ex-husband, and as fate would have it, he is literally under your roof, in your face, every day, so you really have to make peace with him, and all in sight of your present husband."

Sometimes you need a road map to follow Lem's thinking, but I could see that she was right. That didn't mean I liked it, though.

"I don't know why karma is making me find closure with him, or make peace with him at all. He's the one who ruined the marriage, he's the one who said he didn't want to be with me anymore, he's the one who was impossible to live with. I have nothing to apologize for."

"No?" Lem asked gently, reaching for my hand. She laced her fingers through mine. "My love, every relationship has two parts. I don't deny that Robert was horrible to you."

"Ralph."

"Yes. He was a terrible husband and clearly is not emotionally evolved enough to fulfill his end of a successful partnership. But you have to find a way to make peace with the fact that you both contributed to the failure of the marriage so you can move on."

"Move on? I've been married to Sandy for ten years. I think I moved on from Ralph ages ago."

"If you'd moved on, you wouldn't be struggling so much with him living with you guys. He'd be just another annoying in-law. So sort through everything that happened between you, forgive yourself, forgive him, and let it go. Open your heart and just let all the bad blow away. What do you think were your failures in the marriage?"

I didn't respond.

"You don't have to tell me, as long as you tell yourself. Own up to what you did wrong, and let it go. Then let go of everything that he did wrong. Then the slate will be truly clean."

I unlaced my fingers and scowled at her. "I thought you were on my side."

She rose to her feet as the timer on the stove began to beep. She kissed me on top of my head.

"I am," she said.

To Drink, or Not to Drink?

When I got home, I took off my coat, kicked off my shoes, slung my bag onto a kitchen chair and started to reach for the cupboard where I kept my secret bottle. My hand stayed in mid-air as I remembered that not only was it no longer a secret, it was no longer there. Sandy and I had poured the rest of it down the sink together before rinsing and recycling the bottle. Clean and empty, with no more liquor in it. Just like me. I still wasn't convinced I had a full-fledged drinking problem, but if I didn't, I knew I was well on the way to one.

I stood there, looking up at the cupboard where my bottle had been. The thought of not having anything in the house to drink made me feel almost panicked, but I promised Sandy I wouldn't. He'd wanted me to go to AA, but I'd insisted I could do it on my own. If I failed now, I'd never be able to face him. So I took a deep breath, opened the cupboard and took out a box of lasagna noodles. I took some ground beef out of the refrigerator and dropped it into a pan with some chopped onions. I opened a can of mushrooms and grated up a soft chunk of mozzarella cheese. Soon I was lost in the ritual of cooking, of slicing and chopping and boiling and layering. I slid the lasagna into the oven and made a tossed salad which I put into the refrigerator to chill. I washed up, made a cup of herbal tea, tucked a package of Fig Newtons under my arm, then went into my studio.

I turned on the stereo and sat down on my stool. The wrapped clay waited on the table, unmoving, still, waiting for me to bring it to life. I wasn't even sure I had any life left in me to give. I looked up at Brancusi.

"Sculpting used to be my passion," I told him. "My escape. What happened to me?"

For a long time I sat quietly, staring into space, the cup of tea comfortably warm in my hands. I thought about what Lem had said. I thought about Ralph, and about my mother. I thought about how even now, in the safety of a good marriage, I often felt alone, gripped by an imagined abandonment when anything went even slightly off course. Had I driven Ralph away by coiling up inside when he wanted to fight because I thought any unrest would lead to him leave, as my mother had? Would it have cleared the air and made a difference if I'd opened up and fought with him? Or was Ralph just a bully with a big mouth who would have deserted me either way? I wasn't sure of the answer. I wasn't even sure there was an answer. I was still unwilling to let Ralph off the hook, but maybe a bit of the hook did belong to me. Maybe.

I unwrapped the clay, cold and stiff in my hands. I cupped it gently, letting my body heat warm it, sending my spirit into it as I always did. I closed my eyes. A million bits of emotional litter swirled through my mind. I opened my eyes and looked at the clay. Usually I could see what it was going to become, peeking back out at me. This time it was just clay. Just a lifeless gray lump of clay.

A wave of anger started to build inside me, and I threw the clay at the wall as hard as I could. It stuck there for a fraction of a moment, then fell to the floor with a sound like a deflated basketball. The framed Brancusi print crashed down after it.

Slamming the studio door behind me, I grabbed my keys, and went out.

Born to Run

I drove through the streets of San Francisco, feeling rudderless, lost even in the midst of familiar neighborhoods.

I knew I should text Sandy, let him know where I was, but I couldn't bring myself to pick up the phone. For the moment, I was suspended in time, nowhere and everywhere, driving through different parts of the city, passing homes and schools and stores, all full of people who didn't know who I was, didn't know I was there, didn't care where I was going. There's no fear of abandonment when you're alone.

When I got to the Sunset District and found myself on a street I didn't know, I parked, got out and started walking. I passed a bar, warm and welcoming looking, all polished brass and dark wood. As if that had been where I was headed, I went in. It was small, clean and pleasantly uncrowded.

"Anchor Steam, please," I said to the bartender as I sat down. "And a whiskey shot."

"Rough day?" He smiled as he slid the pint glass of beer across the bar and poured Wild Turkey into a shot glass.

"You could say that," I answered, lifting the shot glass in a toast before downing it. "One more."

He poured me another and I knocked it back before picking up my beer.

"Beer on whiskey, mighty risky," I said, pushing the shot glass away.

"Old wives' tale," he said. "Unless you're drinking on an empty stomach."

I considered that. I couldn't remember the last time I'd eaten. I thought about the lasagna I'd left in the oven at home, and my stomach gave a growl so loud the bartender heard it.

"Why can't you have a nice loud bar like everyone else?" I asked.

He laughed. He had a wide, soft smile that underlined his salt and pepper hair and slate blue eyes. I swallowed and looked away.

"Get some food," he said. "The kitchen here is great. How about a bacon cheeseburger?"

"Awesome," I said. The beer was almost gone by the time he went into the back and came out with a plate loaded with burger and curly fries.

"I got you some extra fries," he said. "You look like you need them."

"Do I?" I said. "Do I also look like I need another beer?"

He stuck my glass under the tap while I took a giant bite of the burger, sending cheese and barbecue sauce splattering out the other end.

"Messy," he said, setting the glass in front of me. "That's what makes it good."

Two guys and a girl came in then, and he moved to the other end of the bar to talk to them. I hadn't realized how hungry I was until I started eating. What had looked like an unreasonably large plate of food was disappearing fast. More people came in and sat at a booth in the corner.

"Hey Todd!" one of them called out. "Who do I have to blow to get a drink around here?"

The bartender laughed.

"You're pure class, Adam, good to have you back."

After he'd taken them their drinks, he pointed to my empty glass. I nodded and he slid me another. I was full and warm and, for the first time in ages, relaxed.

"So how was it?" Todd gestured to my empty plate.

"Don't take the plate yet, I still need to lick it," I said. He laughed.

"So are you new in town?" he asked, picking up the plate and wiping the bar with a rag. It was a question I wasn't ready for. I shrugged and looked down into my beer.

"Just passing through," I said. "Heading north."

"Seattle? Portland? Canada? North Pole?"

I got the feeling he knew I was running away from something, but there was no way I was going to admit it.

"Maybe," I said. "I'm just looking for inspiration."

"Inspiration for what? What do you do?"

"I'm a songwriter," I said. Where the hell did that come from?

"Oh cool," he said. "That's awesome. Hang on a sec."

More people came into the bar and he was occupied for a bit mixing drinks and sending orders for mozzarella sticks and potato skins back to the kitchen. I watched him laughing with the couple at the end of the bar as he poured beer and put out bowls of nuts. He was good looking, not stunning but comfortingly attractive, clean cut, with a broad, smooth face and an expression that made him look as though he'd just remembered something funny. He caught me looking at him and winked. I felt my face flush and quickly lifted my glass to block his view. I watched as he talked and laughed with the customers. Obviously this was a favorite neighborhood spot. They all seemed to know each other, and he acted like everyone who came in the door was an old buddy.

Now that the unrelenting tension of the past few months had ebbed, I felt safe, sitting in the middle of this happy, comfortable crowd, but not a part of it. I was used to that, though - the feeling of being disconnected from everything around me, watching my own life as though it was a movie I wasn't particularly enjoying on the only channel that came in.

"So," Todd said, when there was a bit of a lull in the activity. "How's it going over here... uh... I don't think you told me your name."

"Susanna," I said, as he put a fresh glass in front of me.

"So, Susanna, where are you from?" he asked.

"That's it? That's the best you can come up with? You might as well ask me my sign."

"Leo," he said.

I jumped a little. "What? Yes! I am a Leo! How did you know that?"

"Lucky guess."

I narrowed my eyes at him over my glass.

"How come you're so evasive?" he asked. "I barely got it out of you that you're a songwriter who's 'just passing through.' Which, by the way, gives me every indication that you're a writer of county and western songs, and you're going to ride off into the sunset, while a train whistles sadly in the distance."

I laughed, choking on my beer.

"That's exactly right," I said. "It's uncanny how you can read me."

"You don't want to tell me where you're from or anything about you. You on the lam?"

"Nothing that exciting," I said. "Fine, I'll tell you. My name is Susanna Fortner. I'm from Hoboken, New Jersey. I'm a Leo. I write obscure folk songs and travel around, singing in local folk festivals and coffee bars to make enough money to get me to my next stop. I have no family, no history, and more than likely, no future."

"Wow," Todd said. "That's kind of... I don't know. Something."

"Exciting? Glamorous?"

"I was going to say grim, but yours sounds better."

I shrugged.

"It's who I am. It's what I've always done. I'm comfortable with it."

"So how's the songwriting going?"

"Eh," I said. "I'm a bit blocked at the moment."

"Writer's block."

"Something like that. One day I was sculp- writing... a song, I was writing a song, and all of a sudden I just couldn't write anymore. It wasn't there anymore. It was like a door had slammed shut and I couldn't get it open again no matter what I did. So I decided a little road trip would clear my head."

"I get that," he said. "I totally get that."

The people at the end of the bar flagged him down for more drinks, and when he came back, I made a point of shifting the conversation to him. I wasn't sure I'd be able to keep up with the lies I'd told him. It had been disturbingly easy.

"Your turn," I said. "Tell me about Todd the bartender."

He shrugged.

"Not much to tell. I was born and raised in Palo Alto. I went to college in Seattle, then came to San Francisco, got married, settled down, bought this bar from a guy who was selling it and moving to Florida. Pretty ordinary life."

"Ordinary is good," I said. My voice sounded a million miles away.

He shook his head and laughed without smiling.

"That's not what my wife said the night she left. She said our life was boring, that it wasn't what she wanted for herself. Said she didn't want to be a wife and didn't want to be a mother, so she split. Thank God my daughter was barely two at the time, so she never knew to miss her."

I swallowed the tears rising in my throat.

"How long ago was that?"

"Two years," Todd said. "Haven't seen her since."

Another man came around the corner, apparently from the kitchen.

"Hey Todd, you want to take a break before we get slammed?"

"That'd be great, man, thanks. Susanna, you want to keep me company while I smoke a cigarette?"

I was kind of starting to want to molest him, so the dark alley would suit my purposes well.

"Sure," I said, getting off the barstool carefully until I knew my legs were steady.

We stepped into the alley and he let the heavy door close behind him. He offered me a cigarette. I shook one out of the cellophane-wrapped pack, still warm from the body heat it had soaked up in his pocket. He coaxed his lighter to life and I leaned over, slipping the end of the cigarette into the flame. I'd smoked cigarettes before but at that moment, my cigarette and his lighter were the single sexiest thing I'd ever seen.

I leaned back against the building, one foot braced against the wall behind me, and took a long drag.

"Who are you really?" Todd asked, squinting at me through a cloud of smoke. "You aren't really from New Jersey, are you?"

I smiled but didn't answer.

"In fact, I'm going to go out on a limb here and say you haven't told me one true thing about you."

I shook my head and took another drag on my cigarette, not looking at him. I could feel his closeness, the electricity of his skin. I could taste his cologne and cigarette smoke and the faint tang of the ocean in the air.

"Do you know that right now, the only true thing going on is how much I want to kiss you?" he said, his gravelly voice dragging slowly over every part of me.

His face was dangerously close to mine. I don't remember the last time I wanted something as much as I wanted to kiss him. Dropping my cigarette to the ground, I put the fire out with a quick twist of my boot.

"Yes," I said. "And I want to kiss you back. But I'm not going to. Now you can put that overactive imagination of yours to work and come up with the reason why."

Todd laughed, the sound ricocheting off the alley walls like a gunshot.

"You're amazing," he said. "And just so you know, I am going to spend the rest of my life wishing you'd kissed me."

"Yeah," I said. "Me too."

We went back inside just as another wave of people came through the door.

"Will you stick around and keep me company?" Todd asked. "Drinks are on me."

"Sure," I said. "I guess so. Why not."

As he was talking to the new crowd, I pulled out my phone and texted Lem.

"I need to crash at your place later. Pretty sure I'll be coming by taxi." I didn't need to tell her to leave the door unlocked – she never locked it. Half the time she didn't even remember to close it. Then I texted Sandy. "I'm at Lem's. She's having a rough time so

I'll probably end up staying over. Lasagna in the oven, salad in the fridge." I hated lying to him, but right now it was just the easiest way. I had just slipped my phone back into my pocket when the door swung open, bringing a rush of damp evening air and six more people in a laughing group.

"Hey Toad!" one of the men called to Todd. "Did you miss me?"

"Every second you were gone," he called back. "Go away so I can miss you again."

The group roared with laughter. Todd brought me another beer and soon the bar was full. A young guy sat down next to me, his arm around a beautiful blonde girl.

"Hey Frankie!" Todd said. "Sara, how's it going, guys?"

"Good, dude," Frankie said. "Thought we'd come in and hang out for awhile."

"Great to see you. This is Susanna." He winked at me. "She's visiting in town."

"Hey," Frankie nodded to me and Sara gave me a wan smile.

Todd brought them drinks and poured two bowls of peanuts from a big container under the bar.

"Let's get some real food too," Frankie said. "I'm starving. Can we get some nachos?"

Todd disappeared into the kitchen and an awkward silenced wedged itself between Frankie, Sara and me. It reminded me of those giant mechanical animals that played and sang at the popular pizza place when I was a kid. Between sets, they'd gone still and silent, like they'd just died where they stood. Man, those things creeped me out. I toyed diffidently with my glass of beer. To my surprise, Sara spoke first.

"Where are you from, Susanna?" she asked. "I love that name. It sounds so sunny."

"Oh thanks," I said. "I'm from... uh... New Jersey."

"For real?" Frankie was suddenly animated again. "Me too! What exit? Bruuuuce!" He cracked up like it was the funniest thing he'd ever said. Then again, it probably was. Of course, not actually being from New Jersey, I had no clue what he was talking about.

"Haha," I said. "Bruce! Yeah, I'm from Hoboken."

"No way! I'm from Jersey City!"

"No way!"

"Bruuuuce!"

"Bruuuuce!"

"Who's Bruce?" Sara looked annoyed that he and I had an inside joke. I wanted to tell her I didn't get it either.

"Springsteen," Frankie said. "He's a Jersey dude. Kind of a state hero."

I was glad to have that explained to me.

"Yeah, Bruce," I said. "Good old Brucie Bruce."

Todd came back carrying a heaping platter of nachos. It did my soul good to see how fast Skinny Sara shoveled them into her mouth. God bless. Frankie insisted I eat some too, now that we were practically family.

"Hey, you didn't tell me Suz here's from Jersey!" Frankie said to Todd. "She's my homegirl! Hey, let's have some shots! Whiskey, dude. No wait! Tequila!"

Todd obligingly poured out three tequila shots, and Frankie insisted we toast. To Bruce, I guess. I slammed the tequila back, feeling it burning down the back of my throat. I never acted like this, but here, in a place where no one knew anything about me, I had morphed into a different person.

Born to run.

In Bed with Lem

My head felt like it was being split down the middle with a railroad spike and the room was excruciatingly bright. I burrowed down under the covers, which smelled softly of lilac.

Lilac? My sheets didn't smell like lilac. I peeked out from under the blankets just as Lem floated into the room with a cup of something.

"Good morning, my love!" she sang, setting the cup down on the old chair she used as a nightstand.

"Lem," I croaked.

"Yes, my little muffin."

"What's… what? What."

I covered my face with my hands and groaned. Lem perched on the bed.

"I sense you'd like to know what happened last night. Well, I was asleep and I heard you come in, mostly because you fell, and then you crawled into bed beside me, and that was the last sign of life I had out of you until just now."

I closed my eyes and groaned again. Snippets of the night before began to peek into the windows of my brain. The bar, the noisy and friendly crowd, Frankie from New Jersey, Susanna, nachos, Todd… oh God. Todd. I poked around mentally for any evidence that I hadn't changed my mind and made out with him or worse. I didn't think I had… no, I was pretty sure I hadn't. But I didn't remember leaving the bar, I didn't remember getting to Lem's. I definitely didn't remember falling, although given the aches and pains I felt pretty much everywhere, I could believe it. My mouth tasted like nachos and death.

"I brought you some ginger tea with wild honey," Lem said. "Sit up and drink it. You'll feel better. Then we'll have breakfast."

I dragged myself to a sitting position and picked up the cup while

Lem crawled back into bed beside me. She leaned back against the quilted headboard.

"I think I'm starting to show," she said, pulling her nightshirt tight across her non-existent belly. "Can you see it?" Her face was so hopeful that I didn't have the heart to tell her that even through my blurry eyes I could see that her stomach was still so flat it practically went in.

"Yeah," I squinted at her. "Yeah, I think so, a little."

She smiled with satisfaction, one hand resting protectively against her midsection.

"My little butterfly," she crooned, stroking her tummy. "Mommy's little butterfly is so pretty... pretty little butterfly."

Fat, hot tears began to slide down my face. Lem took the cup out of my hand, put her arm around me and pulled me closer, stroking my hair. The tears, held back for so long, came harder and fast, nearly choking me. Good old unflappable Lem just let me cry, humming some random tune that I'm sure was meant to soothe me. Eventually I realized I'd stopped crying.

"Sorry," I mumbled into her nightshirt. "I don't know what that was about."

"I do," she said. "You're angry with Richard for the failure of your first marriage and for pushing his way into your second. You're angry with Sanford for not realizing how you felt and asking Richard to leave. You're angry with your mother for abandoning you. You're angry that the decision of whether or not to have children is being made for you by Mother Nature. Both of those things combine to make you super angry that your whole experience of motherhood has been practically non-existent. My pregnancy is making you revisit all of that, even though you don't want to. You feel as if you aren't in control of anything in your life right now, you can't even sculpt, and the only way you can feel any sense of control is by making your head go fuzzy with alcohol, which dulls the senses but is also a potent depressant so you feel even worse later. Also I think you are developing a drinking problem."

I sat up slowly, my hair stuck to my wet face, and stared at her. She looked back at me, her big blue eyes unblinking. I couldn't get my head around it. Lem, whose psychic abilities were limited to whatever she'd just been told, had touched on things I'd never told her, never told anyone. She'd seen right into my soul and laid out everything I'd been struggling to understand for months, even years. We stared at each other.

"Ralph," I said finally.

"Yes."

The Peaches, Asparagus and Horchata Hangover Cure

Lem wouldn't let me go home until I was ready, physically and mentally, to face Sandy. And probably Ralph. As I showered, she made a big breakfast of bacon and eggs and buttered toast.

"Bacon?" I said, walking back into the kitchen wearing a pair of her yoga pants, which were way too tight, and an old Partridge Family t-shirt. "You're a vegetarian."

"I am, but the butterfly isn't."

"Is this one of those things that makes sense to you but nobody else?"

"It makes perfect sense to everyone," she said, putting about 85 slices of bacon on a plate. "The baby is craving bacon. So when I eat bacon, the baby gets it, but I don't. I'm still a vegetarian."

I took the mug of coffee she held out and took a tiny sip. I was feeling better, but I didn't want to push it.

"So," I asked her, while we ate. "How's River?"

Her face went all melty and she gave me her most beatific smile.

"He's my angel," she said. "He's so good to me and the butterfly."

"Where is he now?"

"He's working."

"Where?"

"In the garden, silly. He's a gardener."

"The garden here?"

"No, not here. But somewhere."

"You don't know where?"

"Why are you asking so many questions, Ari? What is it you really want to know? Just ask me."

"I don't know, I'm just … have you seen him?"

"Of course I've seen him. I'm pregnant, aren't I?"

My headache was coming back with a vengeance.

"I mean have you seen him lately? Does he come around?"

"Yes, he comes to see me every day."

I hoped she was telling the truth, but it was hard to tell with Lem. She never lied, but the things she believed were sometimes wedged in the very tiny crevice between imagination and reality.

"Let's go to the farmer's market," she said, sending yet another piece of bacon to the baby. "I want peaches and asparagus. Then we can go for a nice walk in the park – the fresh air will do you good and I could use the walk. Look at me, I'm big as a barn." She got out of her chair like she was twelve months pregnant.

While she took a shower, I called Sandy.

"Hi babe," he said, his voice cheery as ever. "I miss you."

I suddenly felt like I was going to cry again.

"I miss you too," I said. "I'll be home a little later. Lem wants to go to the farmer's market. I'll get some stuff for supper too – I can make that vegetable stir fry you like."

"That sounds great. If that organic bakery is there again, get some of that sourdough too. How's Lem?"

"She's okay," I said. "It was a rough night last night. She was having, you know, hormone surges and stuff. She's good now."

"That's great. You're a good friend for staying with her."

Guilt hit me in the face and I flinched.

"I don't know how good of an anything I am," I said.

"What's wrong? You sound sad."

"I'm okay, just a little tired. Lem's out of the shower, so we're going to get going. I'll be home this afternoon."

I somehow felt a little better, having talked to Sandy. Hearing his voice centered me, a surprising revelation considering I'd been trying to ditch my whole life lately, especially the night before.

Lem and I took a taxi back to the bar so I could get my car. I put on my sunglasses and tried to keep my head down in case Todd was around. Lem, who had started to waddle when she walked, was taking forever to get in the car. By the time we'd reached the end of the block, I'd started to feel better, and by the time we got to the farmer's market, I felt almost good.

"Did I tell you I think I'm channeling Janis Joplin?" Lem asked as she inspected peaches under the cool overhang of a vendor's tent.

"Uh, no, you didn't mention that," I said, putting zucchini into my bag. "Why do you think you're channeling Janis Joplin? You know you really shouldn't drink or smoke when you're pregnant."

"I don't smoke or drink, Ari, you know that. But there was much more to Janis than drinking and drugs."

"Well, yes, but you have to admit, that's what comes to mind, along with her music, of course."

"I think her spirit is guiding me through this pregnancy, Ari. I can feel her here with me."

I knew better than to argue with Lem when she had that dreamy, satisfied look on her face. It made no sense to me why Janis Joplin would want to hang around Lem while she was pregnant. Janis had been known for her music, and her hard rocking lifestyle that had left her dead on a hotel room floor at the age of 27. But after her swift, and chillingly accurate, overview of my life just hours before, I could no longer immediately discount what came out of Lem's mouth.

She had filled one bag with more peaches than she could carry, partly because she was still waddling. "Here, give me that," I said, taking it from her hands. "Thank you," she said gratefully. "It's just so hard to walk lately." She filled another bag with asparagus, blueberries, basil, tomatoes and some kind of bizarre squash I'd never seen before.

"You expecting company?" I asked. "I wouldn't think Janis eats much these days."

Lem looked at me severely.

"Don't listen to her Janis, she thinks she's funny when she's not," she said into the open air.

"I'm sorry," I said, trying not to laugh. "I'm sorry, Lem. I'm sorry, Janis."

We found a vendor selling freshly made horchata, and it was so amazingly good it helped me get over the last of my wicked hangover, and the embarrassment of having to apologize to the invisible ghost of a long-dead rock star.

"Janis was engaged to be married when she died," Lem informed me. "She had been clean for weeks and was talking about getting out of the music business, settling down, having kids. She died before she could do any of that. That's why she's found me."

"That makes sense," I said. Weirdly, it did.

"So what are you going to do now?" Lem asked me as we sat in a shady spot, sipping our drinks and watching the people.

"I'm going to go home," I said. "I'm going to go home and I'm going to face my demons and I'm going to go to Ralph's wedding, and I'm going to sculpt and get on with my life."

"Smudge," Lem said, slurping her straw loudly in the bottom of her cup.

"What?"

"Smudge. When Rodney is gone, you need to smudge your whole house."

"Ralph."

"Yes. Do you have any smudge sticks?"

"I... no. I'm not even sure what that is."

"Smudge sticks," she enunciated, as though that would make it suddenly clear. When I still looked blank, she sighed.

"Honestly, Ari, it's like we weren't even in the same commune. Smudge sticks are bundles of dried sage you burn to cleanse away bad energy."

"Oh... right. Sage."

"I'll do it for you as soon as he's gone." She patted my leg. "Let's go look at the baked goods."

When she'd filled another bag with sourdough bread, muffins and an enormous apple pie, we headed back to my car. I smiled at all the bags in the backseat.

"What are you smiling at?" Lem asked, huffing a little as she hoisted herself into the passenger seat.

"You," I said. "You just make me feel happy to be alive."

"You should be," she said. "The alternative doesn't sound like nearly as much fun."

I laughed and, on impulse, took out a Janis Joplin CD and stuck it into the player. Lem laughed and clapped her hands. We sang "Piece of My Heart" over and over again on the way back to her apartment and while we were putting her stuff away.

"Lem," I said as I was leaving. "Promise me you really do see this River guy. I haven't seen him around and it worries me."

"You'll meet him. I promise. You're such a fussy Gus." She kissed me and waddled back into the depths of her apartment, leaving the door open as usual. I closed it gently and headed home.

The Pull of the Bottle is Strong for Everyone

The poster of Brancusi, in a new frame, caught a ray of the setting sun, turning the clay on the table from gray to sepia as I bent over my work. The tip of my smallest loop tool seamlessly whisked clay away from an indentation, leaving it smooth. Nearly a month had passed since my drunken half-escape, and life had settled back into a comfortable routine. I hadn't told Sandy anything beyond my original story about spending the night with Lem, but I did tell him I was finally ready to admit I had a drinking problem. I'd gone to an AA meeting the night I came home, afraid that if I didn't face it immediately, I wouldn't.

Now, four weeks sober, I still found myself heading for the cabinet when the sun started to set, and had to force myself to do something else until the urge passed. Not that it mattered too much, there was no booze stashed anywhere in the house.

I had found AA simultaneously depressing and empowering. The support of the others was a relief, but I couldn't help feeling, as I looked around the room on the first night, that we were all confessing, repenting, and giving up, all in one shot. So to speak.

But I was encouraged to know I wasn't alone, that the pull of the bottle was strong for everyone. Another woman had told me one night, waiting with me for Sandy to pick me up, that alcoholism is often genetic. I told her my father never drank, and as far as I knew, my mother hadn't when I was young, but after that, who knows? The Fig Newton thing was definitely her fault, though. Traded one addiction for another, I guess.

I did feel better overall, since I'd stopped drinking altogether. Although he wasn't a big drinker, the always-supportive Sandy had stopped as well, and removed all the liquor from the house, including the million-year-old bottle of sherry with bits of cork disintegrating into it that we only used for cooking, despite my protest that even drunks have their standards. Still, it was hard dealing with Ralph without a drink or four to take the edge off. On the plus side, he wasn't around as much now that he was getting ready to marry Twinkletoes.

Coming home, I realized I'd been more afraid to face the clay than the husband. Sandy was forgiving, tolerant, supportive. The clay was none of those things, and my relationship with it not so easily mended. After two days of avoiding my studio, I'd finally gone in and faced it. Sandy had replaced the broken frame on the Brancusi print and hung it back up. The artist's eyes still watched me, unwavering, to see what I would do. On my confident days, I felt he was issuing me a challenge I was more than ready to accept. Other days, I felt him searching me and finding me lacking. Since I'd returned from that night at Lem's, his eyes were different. Softer. Understanding. He'd fought his own battles and still created art. I would too. The clay acquiesced, pliable now in the warmth of my hands. A form was beginning to take shape but I couldn't yet tell what it was. I just let the clay guide me, allowing myself to get lost in the creative process.

I glanced up when I heard Sandy come home.

"In here, honey," I called. He appeared in the doorway and blew me a kiss.

"I'm just going to run to the bathroom before I pee my pants, then I have something to tell you," he said, jiggling from one foot to the other before dashing off.

"So romantic," I said aloud. I wrapped the clay in plastic and stuck the tools back in their cup. Heading into the kitchen, I washed my hands and made a cup of tea.

"Babe!" Sandy called, zipping past me and toward my studio. I shook my head and smiled. A moment later, he dashed back into the kitchen. "Oh there you are. I didn't see you."

I took out a package of Fig Newtons and sat down at the kitchen table.

"What's wrong? I don't think I've seen you so keyed up since you read that article that said Picasso's wife secretly did all his paintings for him."

"I know, I know, I can't wait to tell you! And that article was total crap, by the way."

I pushed a chair out with my foot.

"Sit," I said. "Have a Newton."

He sat down and took my hand in his.

"Babe, I got great news today. Mr. Somerfield is retiring."

"Mr. Somerfield? As in, your boss?"

"Yes, he's retiring at the end of next month, and babe... he asked if I wanted to buy the gallery."

My jaw dropped.

"Buy the gallery? You buy it? Buy it?"

I've never been particularly articulate when I'm surprised.

"Yes, he said he'd like to know it's in good hands after he's gone. He said he's grown to think of me like a son, and he hopes I'll consider it."

"If he thinks of you like a son, he should just give it to you," I said, stuffing two Newtons into my mouth and spraying crumbs everywhere. Sandy laughed like I'd made the most hilarious joke ever.

"I know! And babe, I think I really want to do it."

I crammed another cookie and took a sip of tea.

"Can we afford it?" I asked.

"Babe, we can't afford not to do it!"

"Ugh, I hate it when people say that. What does that even mean? It doesn't mean anything."

"Ari, listen to me." He took my hand again. My Newton-eating hand. I reached into the package with the other one. Luckily I'm ambisnacktrous. "If we buy that gallery, I can show more of my work, I can show your work, I can do what I've always wanted to do and run a gallery for unknown and new artists. Give them their first break. I think this could be so huge for me. For us."

I studied his face. He was so excited, so earnest, so ready to do this for himself and for me and for the betterment of the entire art world that I suddenly couldn't think of a single reason why not.

"Okay, babe, let's do it," I said. "I'm in."

He gave a whoop and picked me up out of my chair, dancing around the kitchen with my legs dangling like a rag doll. I laughed at his exuberance.

"I assume you'll figure out the whole financial implication of this," I said. "Work something out with Mr. Somerfield?"

"I'll take care of everything and we'll be fine," he said. "The gallery is already established so it's not like I'm starting a new business from scratch."

I put the package of Fig Newtons away.

"Well, I think it sounds like we've got ourselves an art gallery," I said. "Now I think you should take me out to dinner to celebrate."

Lying awake that night, listening to Sandy's soft snoring, I found myself thinking about the half-formed piece in my studio. Finally, I got up, slipped on my robe, and padded down the hall, pushing open the studio door. The plastic-covered clay was fainted illuminated by the streetlight outside. I turned on the lamp and sat down, unwrapping it. In the soft light, I could suddenly see it clearly. I took out my tools, fumbling a little in my excitement, and began to carve, the soft, cool bits of clay falling away as I worked. I worked all night, and by the time the sun found me, I knew I was looking at the piece I was going to send to New York. Inside a hollowed-out sphere of clay, rising from the bottom, was a perfect, intricately detailed butterfly.

Mr. Somerfield, AA and Ch-ch-ch-ch Changes

I stood in the back of the gallery, watching Sandy and Mr. Somerfield negotiate. I lowered my head slightly so I was watching them from between two canvas-bearing easels. Framed by their own artwork. I pulled out my pad and did a quick, rough sketch of it. It wasn't the kind of moment I would ever be able to recreate in clay, but something about it made me want to preserve it anyway.

"Ariel?" Sandy called. "Oh there you are. Mr. Somerfield was asking about your work."

"Sorry," I said, heading back toward them. "I get a little lost sometimes, when I'm around other art. It kind of pulls me in."

Mr. Somerfield, a tall, smoothly handsome man in his 80s, cocked his head just slightly as he looked down at me.

"What were you doing just then? If I may ask?"

"Oh, nothing. I just sometimes sketch things I see that I'd like to sculpt. In this case I don't think it really lends itself to a sculpture, but I wanted to draw it anyway."

I held out my sketchbook a little awkwardly. Mr. Somerfield took it. I watched his face as he looked at the quick and crude drawing I'd done of him and Sandy talking between the easels. I couldn't read his expression.

"May I?" he asked, indicating the rest of the pages.

"Oh, sure. They're not too great, just, you know… sketches."

He didn't answer, silently flipping through the pages. Finally he handed the book back to me and smiled.

"I'd love to see some of your sculptures. Sanford was telling me he wants to display your work here in the gallery. I have to say I'm a little offended you didn't approach me with this before." His blue eyes were twinkling. "Now I'm retiring and he'll get all the credit for discovering you."

I laughed, feeling my cheeks flush.

"Thank you," I said. "I'm really just... I'm kind of an amateur still. I've only had a couple of small shows."

"Do you do single pieces only?"

"Well, yes. Some abstract pieces, some specific things. Heads, faces, plants."

"I would be interested in the outcome if you made a display of several pieces that go together. Like the sketch you just did of Sanford and me."

"I thought about it at one time," I admitted. "But I was afraid it would look too... I don't know. Like a tabletop Dickens Christmas village."

Mr. Somerfield smiled.

"I never like to see an artist give up on an idea before they even try it," he said gently. "Who knows what could result?"

I replayed the conversation in my mind that night as I drove to AA. I had been doing that a lot lately – giving up on stuff before I gave it a fair shake, or any shake at all. Even AA, in a way. I was going to meetings, but I wasn't participating. I had never spoken up, never shared anything. I shut off the ignition and sat there, in my dark car, as that thought broke over me. I was always just doing as much as I needed to do to get by. I never really engaged, never really got close to anyone or anything. I was the closest to Sandy, but there was so much even he didn't know. I suppose a shrink would have said it was because of my mother, who broke the mother-child bond before it had time to fully develop, and also partly because of my father, who had never been a warm and fuzzy man to begin with but became almost a robot after my mother left. I existed, almost entirely, in my own head, skimming across the outside world without really ever touching anyone or anything. Only when I was sculpting did I feel connected to anything, and whatever thoughts and feelings surfaced while I was working I offered up to the Brancusi poster.

"Okay, Ariel, so maybe it's time to make some changes," I said aloud. "Maybe it's time, like right now."

I got out of the car and went into the church's side door, which led directly downstairs, where the group met. A few people were already there, including some faces I'd never seen before. A gray-haired woman in the back row with her head down, a college-aged guy standing by the coffee machine eating cookies, three biker-looking dudes in boots and denim jackets. I nodded to a couple of people who were there every week and found a chair near the front. Shortly after the meeting got underway, I felt myself getting to my feet. Half of my brain was mortified – *oh God, sit down, what are you doing?* – and the other half was cheering that I was finally about to connect to the rest of the world.

"Hi, my name is Ariel," I heard myself say. "I haven't had a drink in a month."

The next thing I knew, I was telling them about my art, about becoming creatively blocked, about Ralph, about Sandy, about running away and getting so drunk I didn't remember even leaving the bar. All around me were faces wreathed in sympathy. No, not sympathy. Understanding. Support. They got it. They may not have understood the feeling of a cold lump of clay that wouldn't yield, but they understood the frustration, the sorrow, the anger that drove me to chuck it at the wall and run for the bar. The gray-haired woman in the back was quietly crying into a tissue, still not raising her head. Others were nodding encouragingly.

"So, I guess that's it," I said. "I just wanted to share and, you know, say thanks for the support I've found here the past few weeks. It's helped. Really."

I sat down and took a deep breath. My hands were shaking but I felt wonderful, as though huge weights had been taken off my shoulders. Getting into the car after the meeting, I shut off the radio and drove home in silence, letting my thoughts fill the car. If this was how it felt to let others in, to connect with them on an emotional level, maybe I could do it after all. Because at that moment, I felt pretty damned good. I couldn't wait to talk to Sandy.

When I walked in the kitchen, Sandy, Ralph and Ellen were sitting at the kitchen table, drinking coffee.

"Oh, Ariel," Ralph said, as though I'd crashed the party. "We were just telling Sandy that we need to stay here for a few weeks while the house we just bought is being remodeled."

Finally Facing Ralph

"No," I said, forcing myself to stay calm.

"What? Why not?" Ralph look irritated and more than a little surprised. "Sandy already said it was okay."

"I'm sorry, but it's not okay," I said. "I know Sandy is your brother but this is my home too, and I am not comfortable with it."

"Ariel, talk to me, don't talk around me," Sandy said. I turned to him.

"Sandy, you told them they could stay here without even talking to me about it first," I said. "You did it while I wasn't even here. So, sorry, but you don't get to tell me not to talk around you. You already talked around me."

Sandy and Ralph stared at me, while Ellen looked embarrassed and uncomfortable.

"Ellen," I said, placing a hand on her arm. "I'm sorry. This isn't about you. I actually like you." I rubbed my forehead and took a deep breath. "Ralph, can we talk?"

"Sure, I guess so," he said. We walked outside and sat down on the porch. I could feel Sandy's eyes on my back as we went out, but I knew what I had to do. I sat down on the top step, hugging my knees.

"Please understand me here," I said. "I married my ex-husband's brother, yes, so maybe some people would question whether I have a right to get upset when my ex comes around. But it doesn't change the fact that sometimes I do get upset. To be honest with you, Sandy and I hit a really rough spot in our marriage after you moved in with us. It wasn't that you were doing anything wrong, but it was just hard for me to have you here. Really hard."

"Because of our history, you mean."

"Well, yes, but it was more than just that. There was a lot of stuff piled on top of that. I hadn't been able to forgive you for everything that went wrong in our marriage, and I couldn't even admit that I'd done anything wrong. It was easy enough for me to hate you during the divorce. Hating you just kind of papered over everything else so I didn't have to deal with it. And then when the divorce was final and I'd moved on with my life, I didn't want to think about it, didn't want to deal with it. And when I married Sandy, it felt like that part of my life, the part with you, was finally behind me and I didn't have to deal with it then because it didn't matter anymore."

I faltered and stopped, my chin on my knees. For once, Ralph didn't speak. Finally I went on. "And then you moved in with us, and I got really, really pissed off. Having you here just reminded me of all the unfinished emotional stuff I hadn't dealt with. And I took it out on Sandy, and I started to drink too much. It was just hard. I was in a really bad place. But I still didn't deal with my feelings, until you brought Ellen here. That night we all went to dinner. I guess that was my rock bottom, as they say. Realizing your ex has someone that makes him happy in a way you never could is one thing, but realizing it with a bottomless glass of wine in front of you takes the whole thing to an entirely different level. That's when I knew I had to face the past, and deal with it once and for all."

"And now?" Ralph said quietly.

I shrugged.

"I'm getting there. Making peace with the ghost of my mother, making peace with you, making peace with just … life. I've got a lot of peace I need to make, and I imagine some of it will take me the rest of my life."

We sat in silence for a few moments. I could hear the sounds of San Francisco transitioning into nighttime. A cricket sang from somewhere under the porch.

"Ralph, I'm sorry for the problems I brought to our marriage. I'm sorry for shutting you out instead of being willing to fight with you. I'm sorry for the anger that was aimed at you when some of it probably should have been aimed at my mother and my father and maybe even myself. There was a lot of baggage I should have unpacked before we got married, but I couldn't. All I did was pack more bags and drag it all home to Sandy later."

There was a long moment of silence before Ralph finally spoke.

"Well, look at it this way. If it hadn't been for me, you'd never have met Sandy in the first place. And as much as I hate to say it, he's a better match for you than I ever was. So... you're welcome."

I laughed. I couldn't help it. Ralph never changes. He laughed too.

"Listen, I'm sorry too," he said. "I wasn't ready to be married and I knew it, but you know I hate admitting when I'm wrong. So I went ahead with it and figured we'd get used to each other. I was a real jerk to you sometimes. You deserve better. And I'm glad you found it."

I gazed out across the lawn, not really seeing anything. I felt Ralph get to his feet so I stood up too. He didn't try to hug me, and I was relieved. I'd taken the first step, but I was still miles away from the finish line. We went back into the house without another word.

"Come on, sweetie," Ralph said to Ellen. "There's a hotel over in Nob Hill I've always wanted to see the inside of. Let's go check in."

The Somerfield

"Well, what do you think?" Sandy said, putting his arm around me. "It's all ours."

"It's all ours," I echoed, looking around the beautiful Somerfield. "I still can't believe it."

"I can't either," he said, running his hand along a marble counter-top. "It looks exactly the same as it has all the years I've been working here, but somehow, there's something different. Just knowing it's mine, it's ours, it's official. Just... wow!" He laughed and turned to me, his face as excited as a little kid on the first day of summer vacation.

"I'm thinking we aren't going to have to do much to the place, just rearrange a little to make more space for new art," he said. "Maybe one wall dedicated to just new artists, unknowns, you know."

"Like me," I said. He laughed and squeezed me. "Yep, like you. I'm so proud of you. I can't wait to show off your talent."

He'd also collected the names of a few other local artists, reported to be very good but still unknown, looking for more of a permanent showcase for their work than small monthly displays in public buildings. The gallery had a longstanding arrangement with some of the area's better-known artists, whose work was always housed at The Somerfield. They would come in a few times a year and add new pieces as others sold. I loved Sandy's idea of making room for unknowns, and not just because I was one of them. My confidence in myself, and my ability to connect with other people had improved by leaps and bounds, but I still wasn't sure I was ready to be in a gallery, especially one with a reputation as good as The Somerfield.

Sandy had already started moving paintings and art glass pieces around.

"I want your stuff front and center," he said, gesturing.

"Oh babe, I don't think I should be at the very front," I protested. "I'm not that good yet."

"What? You're nuts, Ari. You're good and you know it. You're great. And I'm the boss around here now, and I said you're going in the front."

"Favoritism. Or is it nepotism?"

"Yes," he said, kissing me. "There have to be some perks to being the boss's pet."

By the time I stopped in the following afternoon, Sandy and one of the shop assistants had rearranged most of the front of the gallery.

"Babe, look! Here's your spot!" Sandy excitedly showed me several shelves he'd put up at varying heights and widths. I smiled, starting to get excited myself.

"I brought some of my pieces," I said. "They're in the car. Should I go get them?" I felt suddenly, oddly shy. It wasn't until that moment I realized how highly I thought of Sandy as an artist, and how much I wanted him to be proud of me, to admire me, to respect my work as much as I respected his.

We carried three boxes in from the car, then Sandy and the gallery assistants went to work in the back, leaving me alone with my art and my thoughts. Classical music played softly in the background, so apparently Sandy either hadn't figured out how to run the stereo system or hadn't brought his Bob Marley CDs in yet.

I unwrapped the first piece, a child's head I'd made shortly after Ralph and I got married. I ran my thumb over the surface, remembering each line, each curve, each indentation I'd made in the clay, now fired and glazed exactly where I'd stopped. My fingers found the places they'd rested years before, my mind gently returning to those moments, the feeling of the damp coolness in my hands, the features the tools had carved out of the pliant clay. I remembered the way my studio felt, with its dry, forgotten air, the way the slanted attic windows sliced the light into neat pieces before presenting it to me. I remembered the smell wafting up the stairs as Ralph made chili on winter nights. I remembered the way the old rug felt under my bare feet, the gentle, specific warmth of the space heater, the sounds of the Mozart concertos I played while I was working, the distant shouts of neighborhood kids playing football in the park across the street. Those were the moments, I realized suddenly, when I really had been connected to the world around me. All this time I thought I hadn't been allowing myself to connect at all, instead escaping into my art, when all along, my art was what was keeping me tethered to my life. I blinked back tears and smiled softly, putting the piece on one of the shelves.

Two hours later, I was finished. The pieces spelled out a quiet narration of my life, and they looked right, exactly right, in the gallery among all the other breathtaking artwork. Sandy, coming up behind me, wrapped his arms around me.

"That looks perfect," he said, kissing the side of my head. "It's just exactly what I was envisioning for that spot. It's perfect. Perfect."

I had to agree.

Finally Facing my Father

I hadn't seen my mother in years – I wasn't even sure it was her at first, until she came at me with the nail scissors.

"You need to cut that hair!" she shrieked. "Don't you see? They're trying to change you! You have to fight it, Ariel! Show them who you are! Show them you're different!"

She lunged at me with the scissors and I tried to duck, but I felt the sharp pain as the blades closed, chewing through a big chunk of my hair, yanking it, tearing it.

I woke up crying.

"Babe? You okay?" Sandy's sleepy voice found me from across the bed. My hands were shaking, my face and pillow were wet.

"Yeah." I sat up and reached for a tissue. I dried my face and blew my nose, then turned the pillow over before I laid back down. "I was just dreaming that... that Roscoe... ran away."

"Aww," Sandy said. "He's asleep on the floor over here. I can hear him snoring. Go back to sleep, honey. I'll rub your back."

He rubbed my back for about 12 seconds before he was snoring too. I lay awake for a long time, thinking about my mother. I had pushed thoughts of her, all the endless questions I had about her, to the back of my mind for years. Why were they cropping up again now? And why, 40 years after she'd walked out, did I suddenly feel I had to have answers? Deep inside, I knew the answers didn't matter. Not really. Finding out anything I didn't know about my mother wouldn't fundamentally change who I was. It was more a resurgent curiosity about who she was, who she had been, and what had driven her to walk out on her six-year-old daughter, her husband, and her life.

As I lay there, listening to Sandy and Roscoe's out of sync snore duet, I realized I'd never asked my father anything. I remembered worrying about him the day he came home from work and I'd had to tell him she left, and I remembered worrying about him as the days wore on and we realized she wasn't coming back. As months turned into years, I never brought her up. At first he seemed too fragile, too broken. Then, when he started to seem like his old self again, it seemed mean to drag him backward by making him talk about her. So I just never did.

But now it was time.

"What's the point of all these questions?" My father looked irritated. "She's been gone for forty years. What does any of it matter now?"

"I know, Dad, but I just feel like I need to understand a few things. Ultimately, no, none of it really matters, but as I'm getting older there are things I would just like to know. It's all part of who I am and where I came from. Maybe it's part of who I'm becoming. I don't know, but I do know that there's no point in trying to put a puzzle together if you don't have all the pieces."

He stared at me for a long moment, then shook his head.

"Well, you're like her in that respect, I can tell you that much."

"What respect?"

"The infernal questions, trying to figure everything out, and your flair for the dramatic. Puzzle pieces." He shook his head again.

"Really? I don't remember that at all."

"You were six. What were you going to have the answers to? What time Sesame Street started?"

"But what was she like? I remember a little, just bits and pieces, but what was she like before I was born? When you met her?"

He looked down at his hands, and when he raised his head, he had a faint smile on his face.

"The first time I ever saw her, she was wearing a bikini."

I almost fell out of my chair.

"A bikini? I remember her as so straight-laced, almost Donna Reed-like."

"I was working as a lifeguard at the city pool the summer right after high school graduation, and she was at the pool with her girlfriends. They were talking and laughing and walking too fast, so I blew the whistle and told them no running. And she came over to my lifeguard chair and told me she would be happy to make an appointment for me with an eye doctor, because I obviously was too blind to recognize the difference between walking and running. I told her I was the lifeguard so she had to obey my rules. So she said that I should go do something with my whistle that didn't sound like any fun."

I was staring at him, my jaw hanging down.

"The next time she came to the pool, I asked her out," he went on. "And she, for whatever reason, said yes. And a year later, we got married. You never heard that story?"

"No," I said, and laughed. "What a great story."

"She was always very headstrong, didn't like conformity or rules or any of that stuff," he said. "This was the early 60s, so she was a little ahead of her time. If we hadn't gotten married, I suppose she'd have hitchhiked around later with the rest of the hippies."

"But wait, Dad, hang on. I remember my early childhood being very… uh… regulated. I mean, really regulated. That doesn't sound like the mom you just described."

He smiled a little sadly.

"It wasn't," he said quietly. "I'm afraid that was me. I knew she had such free-spirit tendencies, and I was always afraid she would..." He broke off and looked down at his hands again.

"Afraid she would what?" I prompted.

"Run off on me," he said finally. "How about that? Her own parents had been freewheeling beatnik weirdos, and I figured if she had a stable, normal family life, she'd settle down and be able to enjoy it. I wanted her to be happy and, you know… safe. But it wasn't long after she left that I finally got it through my thick head that I'd chased her away. I should have just let her be herself. We'd probably all have been a lot happier."

I guess that explained why the regulation of my life hadn't stopped once she was gone. No doubt Dad had tried, in the only way he knew how, to keep things the same for me so I wouldn't feel unsettled. He suddenly looked very old, sitting there in his worn, green recliner, in the living room he hadn't ever updated, the same books in the same place on the shelves, even the same frame on his glasses. The only thing that had changed were the lenses, the prescription getting slowly stronger as his eyes got weaker. The one part of his life he hadn't been able to regulate was aging. In that moment, I saw him less of the stoic, awkwardly affectionate father he'd always been and more of a human being. A male Miss Havisham, waiting there in the carefully-constructed heaven he'd created, while it slowly became his personal hell.

I blinked back tears and cleared my throat. If I was in this deep, I might as well haul out the big-gun question.

"Dad, did she ever... have a ..." I faltered and stopped.

"Have a what?"

"A... drinking problem."

He looked up at me sharply. "What kind of a question is that?"

"I'm just wondering is all."

"We liked the occasional drink," he said. "Wine with dinner, cocktails when we were out with friends. But no, she never drank excessively. She never did anything excessively. Except cutting off all her hair in the bathroom and walking out on me."

"On us," I corrected him. "And she took the Fig Newtons."

"She what?"

"She took the package of Fig Newtons."

He looked at me blankly. I guess I'd never told him that part of the story.

"When I came home from school that day, she sat me down at the kitchen table like she always did, and she poured me a half-cup of milk and put three Fig Newtons on a plate, like she always did. Then she went into the bathroom and cut off all her hair, and when she came out, she picked up the rest of the package of Fig Newtons on her way out the door. It was a brand-new package too."

My father was staring at me as though he'd never seen me before.

"You never told me that."

"I didn't?"

"No," he said, still looking at me with something like amazement on his face. "Fig Newtons!" Then, just like that, he started to laugh. Pretty soon he had tears rolling down his face and he was gasping to breathe. I'd never seen him laugh so hard. And despite everything, I was laughing too. Finally he got up and went into the kitchen.

"Dad!" I called after him. "Where are you going?"

"I think we need to have a little toast," he called back.

I felt a rising wave of panic. I had never told my father I had a drinking problem, so he didn't know I was sober now.

When he came back into the room, he was carrying two Fig Newtons. He handed me one.

"To Susan," he said, raising his.

"To Mom," I said, lifting my own.

It was the single best Fig Newton I've ever eaten.

Lunch with Twinkletoes McTutu

If I'd woken up that morning with my head glued to the wall, I could not have been any more surprised than I was when Ellen called and asked me out to lunch.

"Uh, well, uh," I responded smoothly. "Uh… okay."

"I know it probably sounds a little weird but we're going to be sisters-in-law, and I'd like to know you better."

"Okay, sure," I said. "That sounds nice."

I was lying through my teeth, of course. I wasn't thrilled about the whole idea, right up through watching her walk toward the table where I was waiting later. She hesitated over whether to shake my hand or kiss me and, after a moment of obviously awkward inner wrangling, sat down without doing either.

"I'm glad you agreed to meet me," she said, fiddling with her purse before putting it over the back of her chair. "I wasn't sure you would."

"It was nice of you to ask," I said. "I was hoping there'd be no hard feelings when I told Ralph you guys couldn't stay with us."

"Not at all. I was actually relieved."

"You were?" This hadn't occurred to me as a possibility.

"Well, yeah. I'd been living in my own place in Chicago for like 20 years. Then he expected me to live in another woman's house and share her kitchen? Her bathroom? And no offense, but, you know… his ex-wife, no less?"

I smiled.

"Yeah, I see your point."

"The worst part is I didn't even know he was going to ask Sandy if we could. He just blurted it out while we were sitting there, and Sandy said yes although I could tell he wasn't too happy. And that's when you came in and put the kibosh on the whole thing, thank God."

"I didn't want you to think it was you," I said. "Since Ralph had been staying with us all that time, and then when he added you to the equation and I said no, I was afraid you'd think it was something against you personally. And it wasn't."

"No?"

"No, it was against Ralph personally." I immediately regretted my words, but Ellen just laughed.

"I get it. I totally get it. I have an ex-husband of my own."

For some reason, this surprised me. It must have showed on my face because Ellen waved her hand dismissively.

"It wasn't worth mentioning. We got married very young. It was an unhappy marriage from the beginning and we split up about ten years ago. But I can tell you this, there isn't a circumstance bad enough for me to ever let him stay with me. Ever. Ever ever ever."

"Yeah," I said. "Exactly. I wasn't thrilled from the beginning when Sandy said Ralph could stay with us, but I didn't push the issue because I felt so guilty."

"Guilty about what?"

"About marrying Ralph's brother. About making the relationship between Ralph and Sandy feel strained."

"Does it still?" Ellen asked. "You've been married kind of a long time."

"It doesn't really, at least not as much as it did. They get along fine and the family has all gotten used to the idea. But there's still that lingering guilt in me, that little voice that says I never should have put their family in that weird position to start with. And I didn't really feel like I could tell Sandy that his own brother couldn't stay with us."

Ellen ran a thin, porcelain finger around the rim of her iced tea glass. I couldn't believe I was sitting here blurting all this out to her, stuff I'd barely been able to tell Sandy.

"I can only imagine the position you felt like you were in, but if it hadn't been for Ralph, you never would have met Sandy in the first place."

"Yes," I said. "That's true. Ralph said the same thing just the other day. And I think Ralph and I have finally made peace."

"He told me," she said. "He thinks so too. I'm glad. I'd like us to be friends if we can."

"I'd like that too," I said, the amiableness in my voice masking what I really felt, which was completely not sure if it was a good idea. Oh well, life was forcing me to do all kinds of stuff lately, and it seemed to be turning out all right.

"So how are the wedding plans coming along?" I asked over grilled chicken salads. I had been eyeing the angus burger and sweet potato fries, but I knew I'd never be able to bring myself to shove that into my face right in front of Miss 80-Pound Ballerina.

"Good. We want to keep it simple and fairly small. Doesn't seem all that important to make it a big white fancy thing, since we've both been married before."

"I felt the same way when I married Sandy, but a lot of women still want the whole princess thing, no matter how many times they've done it."

Ellen wrinkled her nose.

"That seems so pretentious to me. I am just looking forward to being married to Ralph – I don't really care one way or the other about the ceremony itself. I did the whole white wedding thing the first time, and look how that turned out."

I focused all my attention on slicing up a piece of chicken while I contemplated the words "I am just looking forward to being married to Ralph." Nope, still didn't compute.

"I know he's not perfect," she said, apparently reading my mind yet again. "But he's perfect for me."

Impulsively, I reached over and squeezed her hand.

"I'm glad," I said. "I really am."

And that's when I realized... I really was. Good God, when I finally decided to let my guard down and let other people get close to me, this was not what I expected.

Father's Day and a Baby Shower

I'd always dreaded Father's Day when I was a kid, and it turned out I didn't like it any better as an adult. I guess it was a combination of the fact that I don't like holidays that feel made up for the purpose of guilting people into buying gifts and cards, and the somewhat bigger fact that all the years I was growing up, someone invariably asked me what I was doing for my dad on Father's Day, and concluded with "He is both your daddy and your mommy, isn't he?" I never got that. Even as a little kid, their logic didn't ring right in my head. He was my daddy. Daddies couldn't be mommies, they could only be daddies. And I had a mommy, I just couldn't see her anymore. The idea of my father being both daddy and mommy provided me with hours of entertainment as I pictured my stoic, stern father coming home from work, taking off his necktie and wingtip shoes, then putting on an apron and lipstick and making dinner.

My idea of acceptable gender roles is, I think, forgivable when you consider that in the absence of my own mother, the only examples of motherhood I had growing up in the 1970s were my friends' mothers and Carol Brady, a blended bouquet of feminism and tradition in which women went back to work but rushed home as soon as they could, arriving in a cloud of Charlie and polyester before the faint scent of liberation was overpowered by meatloaf and mashed potatoes. When my friends would invite me for sleepovers, I'd often sneak into their parents' bedroom and look for their mother's things – silk nighties, perfume atomizers, tight little compacts of eye shadow as blue as the sky – and marvel that these things were in their house. Because my own mother didn't live with us, they seemed oddly out of place to me, shrouded in thrilling mystery.

"We go through this every year," Sandy said as I grumbled and mumbled my way through my closet in search of an acceptable skirt to wear to brunch. "It's Father's Day, and we are taking your father out. Now behave yourself. You should be glad you have a father. Mine has been dead so long I sometimes have to pull out pictures of him to remember what he looked like."

That last sentence I mouthed along with him. I'd heard it too many times. And it wasn't that I didn't appreciate my father, because I did. But Father's Day just always seemed contrived, forced. I wasn't sure my dad liked it either, but he went because it made him happy to have Sandy pick up the check.

We had just settled down at our table and the waitress had brought a round of the requisite mimosas when my father suddenly cleared his throat, so loudly and theatrically that four people at other tables looked up to see what they were missing.

"I have something to tell you," he said, then paused to drain half of his mimosa. "I'm going on a date."

"You are? Dad, wow! When? Who is she?"

"Her name is Meredith and I met her through someone I work with. I'm taking her to dinner and a movie next weekend."

I stared at him. Earl Carson, my buttoned-down, stern father, whose biggest risk in life had been changing his brand of shaving cream, had actually asked a woman out. I pictured him, nervously fidgeting with his watch, maybe scuffing his toe on the ground as he tried and failed to look her in the eye. Well, whatever he'd said, apparently it worked.

"Congratulations, Earl, that's great," Sandy enthused. "It's about time you were back out there."

It was a ridiculous statement, considering the man had been on his own for almost 40 years, but Dad grinned like a high-schooler.

"Yeah, I'm actually looking forward to it. Ariel, you're okay with this, aren't you?"

I found it odd that he asked what I thought. This was new. All the years I was growing up, I realized at that moment, he'd never asked for my opinion on anything. I looked at him now, smiling uncertainly at me, and realized that somehow, evidently when I wasn't paying attention, everything had changed. And now my father was sitting here asking me for my approval. I smiled and reached for his hand, giving it a squeeze.

"I'm more than okay with it," I said. "I'm really thrilled for you. Happy Father's Day, Dad."

"I think it's great about your Dad," Sandy said later as we walked through the grocery store. I hated grocery shopping with every ounce of my soul, which is why Sandy always took care of it, but he insisted that we get what we needed for the week on the way home from brunch. I told him I had a headache and wanted him to take me home first, but I suspect he saw through the ruse because he responded that if he had to take me home and come back to the store, which was fairly far from the house, he would burn up so much gas that he would be the one with the headache.

"Yeah, I guess it is," I said. "I was just really surprised. He's never even shown an interest in dating before. At least he's never mentioned it."

"There's real healing going on around here, Ari, and I think it's wonderful and amazing. And it's all starting with you, with the good vibes you're putting out in the universe, your new willingness to be open and to connect with the world around you."

"You sound like Lem," I said. "Oh, speaking of Lem, I need maxi pads."

"I'm not sure I see the connection, but okay."

"Oh, she's always trying to get me to use cloth pads like she uses because they're better for the environment."

"I'm sure they are," Sandy said. "You should think about it."

"I'll think about it when I'm not so busy thinking about everything else," I said, stashing a package in the cart. "Like my father dating. I suppose one of these days I am going to have to talk with him about safe sex."

Sandy laughed.

"We could get him some condoms while we're here."

"Don't. Oh man. Gross."

"Why is it gross? He's a normal, healthy man who needs-"

"Stop! I am traumatized enough!"

"You told him you're happy for him."

"I am happy for him. But I don't need to go around envisioning ... stuff."

Fortunately, Sandy's shopping list was fairly short, and we were back in the car before I could feel any real ill effects from having to do the chore I hated most.

"I think I should give Lem a baby shower," I said as we were putting groceries away later.

"That's a great idea," Sandy said, handing me a bunch of bananas. "I'm sure she could use all the usual baby stuff. She probably doesn't have anything."

"Babe, this is Lem we're talking about. I'm sure it hasn't even occurred to her that she needs anything. If I don't get her stuff, the kid will be sleeping in a drawer and wearing a wish diaper."

"A wish diaper?"

"Yeah. You know... I wish I had a diaper."

Sandy laughed and shook his head.

"Do you want to have the shower here?" he asked. "We have enough room, unless you're inviting a million people."

"Half a million," I said. "I think we can fit that many in the living room. I'm going to call Lem."

She received the news with a series of happy little cries.

"A baby shower! I've never had one!"

"No, I don't suppose you have," I said. "Do you have a preference on dates?"

She didn't, of course, Lem has no real concept of time other than the happy, floaty moment she's in. I got my calendar and we chose a date, then made a list of people to invite. I promised her I'd take care of the whole thing, all she had to do was show up and look adorable.

"Get an extra-sturdy chair," she warned me. "I'm huge."

A Silk Wedding Dress and a Hemp Baby Shower

I crumpled up yet another list of shower ideas that had been erased and scratched up into near oblivion. Lem's shower was proving to be a whole lot harder than I'd anticipated, mostly because of Lem. I knew the standard baby shower games she wouldn't care about, if she got the point at all, and wrapping paper, ribbon, paper plates and plastic utensils would culminate in a lecture about the environment and wastefulness. So short of telling everyone to go shop at Cora's and stop off for recycled paper and hemp string on the way home, I had no idea what to do.

I was about to give up for the moment when my cell phone rang. The name didn't come up, but the number seemed vaguely familiar.

"Ariel, it's Ellen."

"Oh, hi. What's up?"

"Well, I need a favor."

"I'm not taking him back, Ellen, a deal's a deal."

She laughed a little awkwardly. Sometimes my sense of humor isn't as finely honed as I want to believe it is.

"No, not that. I was actually wondering if you'd go with me today to pick out my wedding dress. There's a shop over in Telegraph Hill that is holding two for me. I can't decide which I like better."

"And you want me to help you? Are you sure?"

"Yes, I'd really appreciate it. I don't really know anyone here yet, and I like your taste."

My taste? I mostly dressed for comfort and functionality, and I don't remember anyone ever complimenting me on my taste. She must mean my artfully messy house.

"Sure," I said. "I'll come with you, but on one condition."

"What's that?"

"I need someone to help me plan a baby shower for my best friend. I'm having a really hard time because she's not like other women. It's hard to explain. But I could really use a hand with figuring out what to get for it."

"Wow, count me in," Ellen said. "That sounds like fun."

I'm not sure she still thought so when I was in her car an hour later and we were driving toward the dress boutique. After I'd explained about Lem, her quirks, her butterfly, the butterfly's dubious father, and my fears about the baby shower turning into a re-enactment of "An Inconvenient Truth," she didn't seem quite as enthusiastic.

"Well, tell you what," she said from behind her giant Jackie O sunglasses. "Let's get this dress thing over with, and then we'll grab a coffee and kick around some ideas."

"Sure, that's great. And I'm excited to see your dress."

The complete absurdity of the idea that I was going with my exhusband's bride-to-be to pick out her wedding dress was not lost on me, but lately I'd been finding it easier to roll with the punches than to try and punch back.

At the boutique, I immediately understood why she couldn't decide between the two dresses. They were both gorgeous, and on her long, lean, ballerina's body, they both fit like a dream.

"I wish I wasn't so tall," Ellen said, almost to herself, turning back and forth in front of the mirror.

"Yeah, what a curse," I said. "Long legs, long torso, body like a sexy seal... I'm feeling really sorry for you right now."

She smiled a little into the mirror, her eyes still on the dress.

"Thank you, but even ballerinas have things we're insecure about," she said. "No one ever believes that, but it's true. I will probably have to wear flats at the wedding so I don't make us look like the Jolly Green Giant and Sprout."

"I wore flats at mine, but more so I wouldn't fall flat on my face," I said. "Try the other dress on again."

We went back and forth about the pros and cons of each one, and finally decided on a simple silk dress, fitted and mid-calf, in a soft beige color.

"You're going to absolutely knock his eyes out," I told her as the salesgirl slipped the dress into a garment bag. She smiled and twisted her engagement ring, not looking at me. "You're a little nervous, aren't you?"

"A little," she said. "But not because of Ralph. More because of me. I'm devoted to my career, and I hope he can live with it. He says he can, but I guess we'll see."

Over coffee at a little outdoor bistro, we brainstormed ideas for Lem's shower, then did a little shopping to get the stuff we needed. And let me just say this: If you'd have told me six months earlier that any of that would have been happening, I'd have run away screaming. I still might.

Butterfly Kisses

Lem, her little baby bump now pronounced, was wearing a tiara of recycled cardboard, dotted with fake gemstones I'd fashioned from painted clay. Recycled paper banners painted with hemp paint spelled out "Congratulations, Lem" and "Welcome, Little Butterfly!" The mismatched dessert plates and coffee cups that Ellen had found at a thrift store somehow looked absolutely perfect. Janis Joplin's "Pearl" provided the background music. Everyone was wearing butterfly name tags I'd cut from construction paper. The party invitations I'd sent out also had butterflies on them, and the theme apparently stuck.

"Oh LOOK!" Lem cried, unwrapping a pair of tiny booties with knitted butterflies stitched to the toes. "These are the most adorable thing I've ever seen!"

She'd said that about everything she unwrapped, of course, so thrilled with the baby's gifts that she didn't even think to complain about how many trees had been sacrificed for the shiny wrapping paper, or the landfill-clogging curly ribbon. Ellen quietly slipped the wrappings away after each present was opened.

After everyone had eaten the beautifully decorated fairy cakes that Ellen had made and renamed butterfly cakes (I kept starting to wish she would quit being so perfect, but then I'd remember she's stuck with Ralph now), we drank a champagne toast to the butterfly - with sparkling apple juice for Lem and me.

After Ellen and one of Lem's friends had cleared away the plates, I announced a party game I dubbed "Butterfly Kisses." Lem laughed and clapped her hands before she even heard what it was.

"Okay, ladies, here's the deal," I said, holding up two cardboard boxes. "In this box is a bunch of lipsticks. They're all new, so you don't have to worry about germs, I promise. Pull out a lipstick, then take a paper butterfly out of this box. Try not to let anyone else see, but you'll put on your lipstick, then put a kiss on your butterfly. We'll then put all the butterflies into a pile, and the guest of honor here will see if she can figure out whose smackers are whose. After she's done, we'll tell her whether she was right or wrong, and then you can all write messages to the baby on your butterfly, and Lem can have them for her scrapbook."

The party dissolved into absolute hilarity as Lem waddled around the room, holding up butterfly after butterfly and squinting at the guests' mouths like she was investigating a crime scene. She didn't guess too many of them right, but it did my heart good to see how much she was enjoying herself. It occurred to me that I hadn't seen her with a group of people since our commune days, and I was surprised to see how much more animated and involved she was than she had been then. Of course, we were almost 20 years older and didn't smoke weed anymore, but still… there was something different about Lem that I hadn't noticed until that moment. She was connecting to other people in a way I'd never seen before. Always Lem had been among us, rather than one of us, floating in her own plane of existence, a beautiful and fragile fairy that we were afraid to actually touch, lest she shatter or disappear.

I felt my breath catch in my throat as I realized that's what had really drawn us to each other all along – we were both outsiders by our own choice, not wanting to be completely alone, but not wanting to risk getting too close to other people either. Our reasons were our own, but we'd found kindred spirits in each other. And now we were both connecting more, becoming more substantial in our existence, Lem through River and her butterfly, me through my rejection of the bottle and determination to finally face my demons. We were soul mates, Lem and I, and until that moment, I don't think I ever realized just how much that meant.

New York Calling

While having my work officially on display at The Somerfield boosted my confidence a little, it wasn't enough to prepare me for the letter I got two months later telling me my butterfly piece had been accepted for the juried show in New York.

I showed Sandy the letter with shaking hands.

"Babe, that's fantastic news!" he said, hugging me hard. "I knew you could do it!"

My hands were still shaking when I called Lem to tell her.

"Of course you were accepted," she said. "I knew you were going to be. I saw it. Janis knew too."

"Well, thanks for the vote of confidence, to you and to Janis," I said. "Of course, now I'm scared to death."

"Scared of what?"

"Everything. Going there for the opening night event. Meeting all those New York art people. Seeing my piece among all that other art. All that New York art."

"Why do you assume New York art is different from San Francisco art?"

"I don't know for sure that it is, but how could it not be? Look at how different the two cities are!"

"Are they? I've never been to New York. San Francisco is a lot different than Idaho, that I know."

"New York is bigger and, I don't know, older and more sophisticated, I think. I imagine New Yorkers as smart, sharp, competitive, polished, all dressed in black. San Francisco is all fresh air and bicycles and tie-dye."

"I need a tie-dye maternity dress," Lem said dreamily. "Big. A big one. I'm so totally showing now, it's a wonder I can even walk."

I hadn't met River yet, or had any indication that he was even around other than Lem's insistence that he came to see her every day.

"Anyway, I want you to come to New York with me for the opening night party, okay?"

"Oh yes! We would love that. I think my butterfly really wants to see New York."

"I'll book us tickets, you, me and Sandy. Do you think your doctor will let you fly?"

"My doctor?"

"Lem, you have been to the doctor. Please tell me you have."

"You know I don't believe in Western medicine, silly," she said. "I have a midwife."

"Oh, a midwife. Good, that's-"

"She'll bring in a shaman if need be later."

"Oh God."

"My Ariel, you fuss too much. You don't have to worry - I know what's best for me and my butterfly."

She began to sing softly, the disjointed, crooning lullaby she wandered into whenever she started thinking about her baby.

"I'm going to book us tickets to the opening night show," I said to Sandy when I was off the phone. "Lem's coming too."

"Great," he said. He was leaning over a notebook, writing something.

"What are you working on?" I asked, opening the refrigerator to see if there was anything remotely interesting I could make for dinner.

"Just sketching out some more ideas for arranging the gallery," he said. "Minor stuff. When is the opening night in New York?"

I glanced back at the letter.

"September 30. A Saturday."

"Excellent," he said. "It will be a good chance for us to meet some art people on the other coast." He tapped his pencil on the side of his head, always a sign that he was thinking hard. "Actually, that works out really well as it gives me a couple of months to get some names together, contact a few people, introduce myself, let them know we'll be in town."

"Look at you, Mr. Businessman. What happened to the artist who once painted an interpretation of 'The Starry Night' onto a Doritos bag?"

"That was so cool. I should have kept that. I am not in love with the business aspect of art, but I owe it to Mr. Somerfield to keep the gallery's reputation high. And it is interesting to meet people from other parts of the country. If we could get some New York artists to display in our gallery, it would make it more of a draw, maybe even for tourists."

"Tourists don't come to San Francisco to look at art galleries."

"Some do," he protested. "Arty people do."

"True," I said. "What do you want for dinner? I have the stuff for fish tacos – is that okay?"

"Sure," he said, back to writing in his notebook. "Sounds great."

When he was focused like that, I could offer him earth worms on moldy toast and he'd say yes without even hearing me.

"How's Ralph and Ellen's house coming along?" I asked over dinner. "Sometimes I feel a little guilty at not letting them stay here. Not guilty about them, but about you. He is your brother and sometimes I still feel like a kind of homewrecker for what I did to your family."

"You didn't do anything to the family," Sandy said, looking a little surprised. "We're still a family, and you're a part of it. In all honesty, when you stepped in and told them they couldn't stay here, I was big-time relieved. I didn't want them to, but I didn't know how to say no."

"Good thing one of us grew a set," I said.

"Hey now," he said, flicking a piece of lettuce at me. "Watch yourself."

I flicked a bit of onion back at him. He stood up and gestured at the rest of the fish.

"You want I should send you to sleep with the fishes?"

I laughed and started clearing the table.

"If you're practicing for New York, I think it needs a little more work."

"Yeah, fraid so. I'll clean up the dishes. Don't worry about it."

"That would be great, thanks," I said. "I'm going to sketch out an idea for a new piece."

I took my sketchbook and curled up on the couch. I'd been thinking about my conversation with Mr. Somerfield about a display of multiple pieces and had been turning various ideas over in my mind. My father dating, Lem having a baby, Ralph getting married… everything was pushing at my brain, jockeying for attention. I filled several pages with possibilities, but kept going back to one in particular to look at it again. If I could get it to come out like I was seeing it in my mind, it would be a globe, split in two, with water and trees and rocks spilling between the halves, and a woman standing in the middle, atop the debris.

"What is that?" Sandy asked, looking over my shoulder when he came into tell me he was going to bed. I showed him. He studied it for a long moment before handing it back.

"I think there's something really Freudian going on there. Best we don't think about it too much right now."

I glanced back down at the sketchpad, at the exploded earth, at the woman in the middle of it all, before Sandy hit the light and plunged the room into darkness. He was right – best not to think too much about it right now. Or maybe ever.

Lem's Butterfly

"What do you think?" I asked. The moment of silence that followed was just a smidge too long and I whipped my head around to make sure Sandy, Ralph and Ellen were still in the room. Sandy was grinning, Ralph was staring, and Ellen had her hands over her mouth as though she were about to cry.

"It's beautiful, babe," Sandy said. "I can't find a better word for it."

Ellen threw her arms around me, making me stagger backward. I laughed and hugged her back. Sometimes my blossoming friendship with her still threw me off guard, but she seems genuine. And I still think she's way too good for Ralph.

"It's amazing," she said, sniffling back tears. "I've never seen anything like it."

Even Ralph grudgingly mumbled something positive. I looked at the piece spread out on the table in the living room – I may have been more connected to the rest of the world but I still didn't like people being in my studio – and saw it again, this time through their eyes. I'd sculpted a woman, very small, then several variations of her, increasing in size. One was climbing over a fence, one was scaling the side of a mountain, one was swimming, and the final one was standing atop a rainbow, her arms reaching skyward in victory. It was personal, but it was more than just for me. It was for me, it was for Ellen, it was for Lem, it was for my mother... it was for every woman who has ever had to fight to get where she wanted to be, for all of us who wanted nothing more than to be able to raise her arms and know she made it.

My cell phone rang, buzzing loudly against my sculpting table. My hands still had clay on them, so I motioned for Sandy to grab it.

"What?" I heard him say. "Slow down. Say it again."

When he looked up at me, his eyes were big and his smile was bigger.

"Lem's in labor!"

"What?! She's not due for another two months! Oh my God! Is she okay? Where is she? She's early! I have to go!" I literally ran around the room in a big circle, trying to remember where my bag and keys were. Sandy reached out and stopped me.

"She's fine. The midwife is with her. They're at Lem's – apparently our girl decided on a water birth. It sounds like the baby is coming fast."

"A WATER BIRTH?! In that dinky little bathtub in her apartment? WHAT THE HELL IS WRONG WITH THAT MIDWIFE?! I have to go. Call an ambulance, we'll meet it there."

"Ari, calm down," Sandy said. "You can't send an ambulance to Lem's if she doesn't want one. She has a good midwife, and she'll call the doctor if they need one. Let's just go."

"Yes, let's just go," I said, grabbing my bag and, without realizing it, Ellen's hand. We all piled into our car and Sandy sped toward Lem's.

"I didn't even know Lem was pregnant," Ralph said from the backseat.

"Yes you did," Ellen said. "I told you that. We threw her a baby shower? Remember?"

"Oh, right," Ralph said, clearly lying through his teeth.

"I can't believe she's in labor! She's been so healthy and fine all along and now she's in labor eight weeks early! Oh my God, I'm so worried about her!" I wailed.

Sandy squeezed my hand.

"She'll be fine," he said. "We're almost there."

"Who's the father?" Ralph asked. His very presence was beginning to bother me at that moment.

"Her boyfriend," I said, doing my best not to snap at him. "He's a great guy. Really good to her." Well, Lem said so, I told myself, and right now that was good enough for me.

"Well, good for her," Ralph said, then began to talk to Ellen, clearly having lost interest.

Sandy pulled the car to a stop in front of Lem's building and I jumped out of the car and ran inside faster than I've ever run, leaving everyone else behind. I took the steps two at a time and threw open the door to Lem's apartment.

"LEM!" I shrieked, and stopped dead in my tracks. On the sofa, Lem lay looking positively beatific. Next to her was a man with long brown hair, a neatly trimmed beard, huge dark eyes and a smile as wide as a mile. In her arms was a minute, slightly damp infant, busily nursing. Janis Joplin was playing quietly on the stereo in the corner, quietly for Janis anyway.

"Ari!" Lem said, looking up at me with a face full of wonder and love. "Look at my butterfly! It's a girl!"

I dropped to my knees beside the sofa, tears streaming down my face. I kissed Lem, I kissed the baby, I kissed a very surprised River.

"She's beautiful," I said, gently touching the fuzzy little head. "You're all beautiful. I'm so glad everything is okay."

I felt a hand on my shoulder and looked up to see Sandy.

"Hi Lem," he said softly. "Congratulations."

Her beam lit up the whole room. "This is my butterfly," she said, introducing the baby to Sandy. "And this is my River."

The men shook hands.

"Congratulations, man," Sandy said. "This is awesome."

"It really is," River said. "I'm blessed. We're blessed."

"Lem, there are a couple of people in the hallway who want to give you their best but if you think you're up to it. We will only stay a minute."

The midwife came in from the bathroom as Sandy was finishing his sentence.

"Not too many people," she cautioned. "Preemies are a little delicate."

"We'll be out of here fast," Sandy promised. He went to the front door and let Ralph and Ellen in.

"Hi Lem," Ralph said when he saw her.

"Hi Roger," she replied, her eyes on her baby.

"Ralph," he said.

"Yes."

"Hi Lem," Ellen said softly. "What a beautiful butterfly!"

"Thank you, Ellen," Lem said happily, her eyes still on her baby. Ellen discreetly pulled Ralph away, mouthing to me that they would wait in the car.

"I was so worried about you, honey," I said, laying a hand on Lem's soft blonde hair, unable to stop the tears.

"I know you were, Miss Fussy Face," she responded, then looked up at River. "I told you, didn't I, how she fusses over me?"

"You did, my love," he said, crinkling a smile at me. "I'm glad. I'd be here every moment if I could, but I've been putting in extra hours to build up a little nest egg for us. I'm glad she has you to lean on when I'm not around."

Sandy nudged me to my feet.

"We're going to go now so you can rest," he said.

"I'll be back to see you soon," I said, kissing Lem again.

"My door is always open," Lem said, non-ironically.

As soon as we were outside, Sandy put his arm around me and I burst into a fresh wave of tears. He held me while I sobbed. I cried with relief that Lem was okay, I cried with happiness because River really did exist, I cried because the baby was so beautiful and tiny, I cried because I maybe really did want a baby of my own, I cried because Ralph was sitting in the backseat of my car.

Feeling Stronger Every Day

It didn't occur to me how impressive it was that I'd gotten through the talk with my father, lunch with my ex-husband's fiancée, the news about the art show in New York, and the premature birth of Lem's baby without so much as one drink until I recounted everything at AA later.

"So you broke down and had a drink?" a man on the front row asked when I'd finished my story. I looked down at him in surprise.

"No," I said. "I actually… wow. No, I didn't. I didn't even think about it."

Everyone applauded except the gray-haired woman in the back who, as usual, had her head down. The only time she ever moved was to dab at her eyes with a tissue. She never spoke, never socialized with anyone. I'd only caught one fast glimpse of the side of her face one night as we were leaving, and she wasn't close enough for me to talk to. I felt oddly drawn to her, like I wanted to help her or at least hear her story. I kept hoping she'd stand up in a meeting and share, but she never did.

"That's great," the program leader said, when the applause died down. "I think what's most encouraging about what we just heard is that you didn't even wish for a drink. That's bigger than you probably even realize."

"Yeah," I said, still a little amazed at it myself. "Yeah, I'm glad. I feel much stronger than I did when I first came here. Maybe stronger than I've felt in my whole life. And it's funny, but even when I picture myself at the art opening in New York in September, at the cocktail reception, I know I can get through it with a club soda in my hand."

Heads nodded, and there was another smattering of applause. I sat down, suddenly aware of how much I'd been talking. Wow, I didn't even know who I was anymore.

Willow smiled up at me and waved her hand in that kind of spasmodic, involuntary way that babies do, then laughed at the sheer absurdity of her own free-thinking arm.

"She's so smart," I said to Lem. We were sitting on the grass in the park near her apartment. We both had our legs stretched out in the sunshine. River was planting flowers nearby, pausing every now and then to look over at Lem with a big dopey smile on his gorgeous, tanned face.

"Yes, she is," Lem said, looking at her with wonder. "I still can't get my head around the fact that this is a person. Her own self, a small person who was inside my body just a few months ago. It just blows my mind."

Willow laughed again, a tinkling squeal that made me feel like nothing could ever go wrong again.

"She agrees with you," I said, lightly tickling her tummy with my fingers. She made a gurgling sound and kicked her feet excitedly. "You agree with Mommy, don't you? She definitely has your sunny disposition."

"It's her own disposition," Lem corrected me. "I still have mine."

"Oh right. Of course. Silly me. And here I was going to say she's smart like her Mommy and her Daddy."

"She's very smart. River is smart too."

"He seems it."

"I never bothered with college, but he loved it. Graduated top of his class."

"Wow," I said. "Where did he go to school?"

"M... something. Some school out in Massachusetts."

My hand froze mid-tickle over the baby.

"MIT?" I asked.

"Yes! That's it. Mitt."

"He graduated at the top of his class from MIT?"

"Yes he did. Didn't you, love?" She addressed the rest of her comment to River, who had just come over to check on everyone.

"Didn't I what?" he asked, kissing her.

"Graduate from Mitt?"

"Yeah," he said. "Good old Mitt."

"What did you get your degree in?" I asked curiously.

"Earth, Atmospheric and Planetary Sciences," he said.

"Your... master's?"

"Doctorate," he said.

"Doctor River!" Lem said in a sing-song, feeling around under her legs for her water bottle. Willow began to squawk and Lem got up.

"I hope you don't mind my asking," I said to River. "But if you have a PhD from MIT, why are you a gardener?"

He shrugged and smiled.

"Because I like it."

Ask a stupid question...

"Good for you," I said, watching as Lem wandered down by the water, rocking Willow in her arms and crooning softly. "I'm also glad you're, well... here. When Lem first told me about you, I wasn't sure you were the real deal."

"How so? You mean you were afraid I'd knocked her up and then disappeared?"

"Well, yeah. I mean, she was pregnant and I never saw you. She kept telling me you came to see her all the time, and she seemed very happy, so I really did try to believe her. It was just hard. It all seemed a little far-fetched."

"Lem told me that was your ex-husband who came to see us right after Willow was born."

"Yes. Ralph. It's just a bizarre situation all around."

"Lem told me. It's not as bizarre as you might think, but it doesn't sound like you and he had the best marriage, if I can say so."

"That's the understatement of the millennium."

"So is it possible you were hauling around the unspoken assumption that all men are assholes, genetically programmed to break hearts?"

"I don't know. Maybe. I have a good marriage now."

"Yes, I can tell. But if you haven't made peace with what happened in your first marriage – and some people never do, so not judging – it is pretty much impossible to see past it, no matter how good your current marriage is. At some level, you probably view your second marriage as an anomaly, or a fluke, or a stroke of good luck, but that your first marriage is the one that's really indicative of how most relationships are."

I didn't answer for a moment, just concentrated on flicking a blade of grass back and forth with my index finger. Finally I spoke.

"I did make peace with Ralph, eventually."

"I'm guessing that was... recently? After you found out Lem was pregnant?"

"Yeah."

He nodded.

"That sounds about right."

"What are you doing, analyzing me? I thought you said your degree was in moon rocks or something, not psychology."

"I just find the human mind fascinating," he said. "I do a lot of reading."

"Okay, I'll bite. Why did you say it sounds about right that I made peace with Ralph after I found out Lem was pregnant?"

"Oh, it's just an observation. I don't have any scientific or psychological evidence to back me up, but I've noticed that whenever a baby is on the way, people tend to want to clean up. It's the same phenomenon that causes mothers-to-be to start nesting. Sometimes it manifests itself through people wanting to mend fences, clear out emotional clutter. I like to think it's because everyone around wants to do whatever they can to try to make the world a little better for the new life that's coming in. And in your case, you and Lem are like sisters, so this baby is as much family to you as if there were blood ties. I think it shows what an amazing, selfless person you are. And I, for one, am glad you let me into your family."

I smiled at him. He'd been a stranger to me just a few months ago and now, he was right, we felt like one big family.

"Me too," I said. "Really glad."

"Want to know a secret?"

"Sure," I said. "I keep secrets like a boss."

"I'm going to ask Lem to marry me."

I let out a squeal and then clapped my hand over my mouth, but Lem was too far away to hear.

"Oh wow! Oh, I'm so happy! Oh that's so awesome!" I waved my hands in front of my face. Good God almighty, all I did these days was cry. "When are you going to ask?"

"I'm not sure," he said. "Soon."

He wasn't kidding. Lem called me at home that night, laughing and crying so hard she gave herself the hiccups.

"Marry... River... me... Ari! Yes!"

"Oh Lem, I'm so happy for you! I'm just so happy for both of you, for your sweet little family. This is just perfect. Have you talked about a date?"

"Hang on." I heard her put the phone down and blow her nose loudly. "That's better. We want to do it soon, like this fall. In the next few weeks. Now. I want to ask you two things."

"Shoot."

"Number one, will you stand up with me? It's going to be a really small ceremony, with just a few friends, but I really want you to be my honor maid. Maiden. Honor. Maiden of... shit! Just, will you?"

"Yes, of course, my love. I'd be honored and thrilled to be your matron of honor."

"Matron? That doesn't sound right. Matron. Maaaaay-tron."

"Lem!"

"Yes?"

"You said you wanted to ask me two things."

"Yes. The other thing is do you mind if we both come to New York with you? I really want to be there for your art show, of course, and we thought we'd just stay and have a little honeymoon there afterward, before we fly back."

"I think that's a great idea! I'm so excited about all of this, I am freaking out right now."

In the background, I could hear the baby starting to shriek, so Lem rang off and I ran to tell Sandy the news.

"Wow, that's great," he said. "Everything is really rocking and rolling around here lately."

"Yes," I said. "It is. It really is. I think I'm going to go into the studio for awhile before dinner, if that's okay with you."

"Sure," he said. "I'm going to be working on the gallery's mailing list out here, so if you need anything, just whistle. You know how to whistle, don't you? You just put your lips together..." he puckered up.

"And kiss me," I said, kissing him.

In my studio, I turned on the lamp and the stereo and lit a candle. I sat down on the stool next to my sculpting table. A new block of clay, smooth and shiny under its plastic exoskeleton, waited with an expectancy I could feel. My tools, jutting up like pointy flowers from their terracotta pots, still had dried bits of my last successful project clinging to them. Above me, I could have sworn Brancusi's expression had changed – there was a slight crinkle at the corners of his eyes I had never noticed before. I could hear Sandy humming something to himself, off-key, in the other room. We don't get those moments of absolute, perfect peace very often, but in that instant, I found mine.

The Bamboo Wedding Dress

"What do you mean you don't want a wedding dress?" I asked Lem. "What are you going to get married in? Overalls?"

"No, but... actually that's a cool idea."

"Lem!"

"Oh okay. But no, I'm not doing the whole white dress bit. I don't want any of that. It's ritualistic, materialistic nonsense that has nothing to do with marriage at all. In fact, if wedding tradition truly embraced what marriage really is – merging yourself body and soul with another person, and loving and being loved for who you really are – we would all get married completely naked."

"You wouldn't dare."

"Mmmm. We can't get time in the garden at the nudist resort on such short notice."

"You checked?"

"Of course I checked, silly. It's such a beautiful idea. I can't imagine why more people don't have naked weddings."

"Yes, it's a real shame that never caught on. It would be a whole lot easier than trying to get shoes dyed to match a bridesmaid's dress."

"Ari! You think so too! I heard there's another resort not too far away, I could call!" She started to dig for her cell phone but I stayed her hand.

"Stop, I was just kidding. But you do need something special to wear, Lemmie, it's your wedding day!"

"I want something floaty, pretty, made of renewable fabric – no silk!"

"No silk."

Lem snapped her fingers.

"I know!" she said. "Let's go see Cora!"

"Cora? Cora of the three dozen naked kids? Cora who is the modern embodiment of the Old Woman Who Lived in a Shoe?"

"Yes!" said Lem happily. "Cora will fix me up."

River was out at the garden center, so we loaded Willow into the car and headed out. This time when we pulled into the driveway, I was glad to see that none of the kids who were hanging from the tree or the eaves were naked. It was getting a bit chilly for that, and anyway now I was afraid that Lem would drop trou and join them.

Cora hailed us joyfully.

"Lem and Ariel! How nice to see you again, and oh my word is this your butterfly?"

"Yes," Lem said happily, lifting the blanket off the infant seat so Cora could see inside. "This is Willow."

"Oh my heavens, she is precious, and so tiny!"

"She came early, by two months," Lem said. "But she eats like mad and is growing so fast. I don't think she's a vegetarian. She likes bacon." Cora, understandably, seemed about to say something when the back door slammed and a chunky boy of about eight thundered through the kitchen and up the stairs. In the distance, we heard another door slam.

"Coincidentally, that was MY preemie baby," Cora said. "If that gives you any hope at all."

This made us all laugh, and Lem set the infant seat down.

"So what can I do for you?" Cora asked. "Baby toys? Blankets?"

"No, I need something for me," Lem said. "I'm getting married and I want a dress, but I want something special. Something very me."

"Organic fabrics, ethereal, gauzy, floaty, humane, sustainable," I added.

"And yellow," Lem said, nodding.

Cora's smile was threatening to divide her face in half.

"I have just the thing," she said. She went into another room and came back a few minutes later with a bolt of soft fabric.

"I can easily dye this a pale yellow. I have a whole bunch of organic dyes."

Lem felt the fabric.

"Wow, so soft. What is it?"

"Bamboo," Cora said. "We make all our own fabric."

"Bamboo is highly sustainable," Lem mused. "Is it locally sourced?"

Cora pointed.

"Right there in our backyard. How's that for local?"

"Oh that's perfect!" she said. "Can you make me a dress in a week?"

"Absolutely," Cora said. "Let's just take your measurements."

While they measured and talked about sleeves and necklines, I wandered back into the shop. Walking among the tables, I trailed my hands over baby blankets, booties and tiny sweaters. The arms were tiny, the buttons were tiny. I picked up a pale pink one and held it to my face, inhaling deeply. It didn't smell like a baby, of course, as a baby hadn't worn it. Funny, though, I instinctively expected it to smell of talc and baby shampoo. As I put it back down on the table, I glanced up and saw all the delicate glass butterflies swaying gently from the ceiling, sending showers of colors over the shop whenever they'd catch the light. And that's when I knew what I was going to give Lem for a wedding gift.

After a whispered conversation with Cora while Lem was putting Willow into the car, it was all arranged.

Lem Gets Married

As it turned out, the best gift she got was the weather. The day opened with perfect autumn sunshine and cool air laced with just enough warmth. The trees were beginning to think about changing colors but hadn't fully committed to it.

I arrived at Lem's early under the guise of helping her get ready, although secretly I just wanted to make sure she didn't default to the naked plan at the last minute.

She was wearing a pair of panties, which I guessed was a good start, and brushing her teeth when I walked in. Willow was lying on a blanket on the floor, waving a rattle around with one hand and staring at it in smiling, toothless wonder. I sat down on the floor beside her and patted her tummy.

"Are you nervous?" I called to Lem. I heard the water shut off and she came out of the bathroom.

"No, why? Should I be?"

"No, I guess not," I said. "Some brides are."

"I'm just happy," she said. "I love River from a place I never knew existed. Between him and Willow, I'm experiencing a level of love that really shouldn't even be described as love. It's more than that. It's so much more."

She hugged me hard.

"Now," she said. "Let's get that dress on. Wait until you see it. It's a dream. It's a floaty, hemmy, Lemmy dream. Hang on, I'll go put it on."

She went back into the bathroom and emerged a few minutes later, a vision in a pale yellow dress that fell flatteringly over her slim body but showed just enough of her temporarily large breasts to be really sexy.

"That is amazing," I said. "That dress was made for you."

"Of course it was," she said, looking puzzled. "You were there, remember?"

"Yes, I know. I just mean... you look amazing, Lem. Like a fairy princess."

She gave a little twirl, making the handkerchief hem flare out. It doesn't matter how old a woman is, if you put in her a dress with the right kind of skirt, she's going to twirl. It just can't be helped. It's out of our control.

"Oh, wait till you see what Cora gave me as a gift!" Lem said. She went into her bedroom and came back with the cutest little wood nymph dress I'd ever seen. All greens and purples and blues, soft watercolors, with little matching booties and a hat. I clapped my hands over my face.

"I can't take it," I said. "That is the most adorable thing ever. Is she going to wear it for the wedding?"

"Yes! Let's get her dressed!"

Between us, we got the squirmy baby into her new outfit. She looked like a tiny naiad. I snapped pictures with my phone until Lem finally grabbed it out of my hands.

"Let's go, or River will think I'm not showing up!" she said. "I just got nervous! Oh my God, I just got nervous! I'm getting married! Ari!"

I laughed and hugged her.

"You're getting married! Let's do this thing!"

I loaded the fairy princess and her miniature wood sprite into my car and we headed for the spot they'd chosen – a big flat rock near the water, with the Golden Gate Bridge as the backdrop. River's face lit up like a beacon when we drove up. When Lem got out of the car, I thought he was going to cry. He hugged her for a long moment, so long I was starting to feel like a voyeur. I got the infant seat out of the back of the car, and when he saw Willow, he really did start crying. I handed the baby over and left them to their family moment. Sandy was standing under a tree near the water, smiling as I approached. He kissed me and pulled me to lean against him as he leaned against the tree.

"It's nice here," he said.

"Mm, very. I love San Francisco so much."

"You're not ready to abandon it for New York?"

"Hardly. I am looking forward to seeing New York, but this is the only place I would ever want to live."

"Yeah, me too." He rested his cheek on top of my head.

"Who else is coming?" I asked. "Do you know?"

"River said just a few other people, some other friends of his or theirs. Not sure which."

"No chairs or anything?"

"River said that according to Lem, everyone is going to sit on the ground. Something about communing with nature and the spirit of love."

"Lem was always a better hippie than I was," I said.

"She's a better hippie than all of us," he agreed. "Do you have your present ready?"

"It's in the backseat, covered with a sheet so she wouldn't see it," I said. "I knew she'd be too distracted to notice. I'll go move it outside the car so it's not too hot."

"Put it over here by the tree. She won't see it. That way you can get to it easily."

Within a few minutes, the other guests had arrived, as well as the minister, an elderly Native American woman in an embroidered skirt and Birkenstocks. I felt like I was back at the commune. We all sat down, the minister on the rock with the water behind her. Lem and River sat directly in front of her, Willow on River's lap. I wished I'd brought my sketchbook – they looked so perfect. I tried to memorize every line, every feature. This was a scene I absolutely had to sculpt.

"Friends, thank you for being here with us as we celebrate the creation of this family, this sacred union. Lisa-"

"Lem," the bride interrupted. "My Native American name is Lemon Wax. But please call me Lem."

"Lemon... Wax? Is your... native... uh... okay..." The minister, completely befuddled, looked at River, who just laughed. Then everyone laughed, including the minister.

"Amid this laughter, this friendship, amid these gifts of nature and man, we ask for blessings upon this union," she said, raising her hands. "The universe has brought Lem and River together, and through them, has created another beautiful life. Now we offer up this family to the Great Spirit, to the universe, to every sacred soul who watches over us as we walk this earth. Lemon Wax, is this man your soul's true mate?"

"Yes," said Lem. Her voice was almost a whisper.

"And River, is this woman your soul's true mate?"

"Yes," River said.

"Then by the powers vested in me by the Great Spirit, Mother Earth and, to a much less important degree, the state of California, it is my great joy to proclaim you husband, wife, and family." The minister shook something from a small vial onto her hand and touched first Lem's head, then River's, then Willow's. River leaned over and kissed Lem, and everyone began to clap and whistle.

Sandy went over to the tree and picked up what I'd hidden – a wicker cage full of butterflies. I opened the door and almost immediately, the sky over us was awash in color and fluttering wings. Lem whirled around with a squeal and saw the now-empty cage in my hands. She flew into my arms, laughing and crying, and everyone gathered to watch the butterflies take flight over the water and the bridge.

It was without a doubt the oddest, most creative, most beautiful wedding I will ever see in my life. In other words, it was Lem all over.

"The butterflies were a nice touch," Sandy said later as we were getting ready for bed. "I didn't think they encouraged people to do that at weddings anymore. I thought it messed with their migratory habits."

"It isn't generally a good practice," I answered, trying to coax Roscoe from the middle of the bed. "But that day we were getting Lem's wedding dress, I asked Cora what she thought of the idea. She's a big butterfly enthusiast so I figured she'd know. It turned out she collects caterpillars native to this area so she can be sure they're safe from pesticides and stuff, and when they turn into butterflies, she releases them. She had a bunch that were just about ready, so the timing really worked out perfectly. Did you see Lem's face? I will never forget that as long as I live."

Sandy leaned over and kissed me.

"It's your face I'll never forget," he said. "You looked even happier than Lem did."

I thought about that long after we shut the light off. Butterflies were becoming a recurring theme in my life, and the memory of all those tiny, strong wings taking flight in the California skies filled me with peace. Peace and, Sandy was right, happiness.

Start Spreadin' the News...

I expect we were one of those groups of people that make other travelers offer up the frantic, silent prayer of "Please don't let them be sitting near me!" when they spot them in the airport terminal. Lem, whose hair was now light purple, crooning "Me and Bobby McGee," Willow dressed in a tie-dyed onesie and squalling out her disapproval of her mother's song choice, River, his guitar case at his feet, talking earnestly to Sandy about the United States' policy on Israel, Sandy animatedly disagreeing, and me quietly having a nervous breakdown.

I honestly had no idea how they could all be so calm when I was about to make my artistic debut in New York, where I could easily be laughed right out of town. What was I doing? Who did I think I was fooling? I wasn't an artist, not of this caliber. My art was meant to be mostly just for me, a creative outlet, a soothing pastime, an enjoyable hobby, definitely not meant for anything larger than a local show or two, or my little space at The Somerfield. But I'd gotten lucky with one piece and New York had noticed and now I had to go stand there and listen to people talk about it and ask me questions and expect me to answer like I knew anything about art, when all I really wanted to do was run back to my studio and close the door and talk it over with Brancusi. And have a drink. Man, what I wouldn't give for a drink. I looked longingly at the nearby bar, where people were relaxing with a pre-flight cocktail. I could see for myself how much it was taking the edge off for them, while out here, my edges were becoming more and more prominent. I'd be a giant, human trapezoid soon. I moved to a different chair where I wouldn't have such a clear view of those people I now hated. I reached into my bag where I'd stashed a package of Fig Newtons and put two in my mouth at once.

"You okay?" Sandy sat down beside me. I nodded and gave him a thumbs up since I couldn't speak without spraying fruit and cookie everywhere.

"I don't think so," he said. "You only put two Newtons in your mouth at once when you're stressed out."

I swallowed and took a sip from the cup of tea he was holding.

"I'm okay overall," I said. "Just a little nervous. This is kind of a big thing, this New York art show, and I'm still not convinced I'm a New York-caliber artist."

"You think a lot of the New York art world for someone who doesn't know that much about it. Why do you assume they're so much more awesome than the San Francisco art world?"

It was a valid question. I shoved two more Newtons into my mouth instead of answering. Sandy laughed and put his arm around me, giving me a squeeze.

"You're New York-caliber or they wouldn't have chosen you," he said. "Now relax. Can I have a Newton?"

I eyed him.

"Will you keep sharing your tea?"

He held out the cup and I gave him a Newton, then gave him a second one because he looked so cute. By the time we boarded the plane, I felt a little better. I generally hate having the middle seat, but in this case, I found it calming to have Sandy on one side of me and Lem on the other. River was across the aisle, ostensibly so he could help with the baby when Lem needed a break, but I was also pretty sure it was because he knew I needed the comfort of my friend close to me. Sandy once compared her to the goat a rancher will sometimes put in with a horse to calm it down. Good old Lem. She was my goat.

"Will you hold her?" Lem said, plopping Willow onto my lap so she could make a bathroom run before the plane took off.

"Now why would I want to hold you?" I said to Willow, who gave me a small smile in response. She had a funny way of giving a half smile and a look out of the side of her eye that always made her look as though she didn't quite believe whatever was being said. "Why would I want to hold you? You think you're special?" I tickled her tummy and she reached up and touched my chin. For a moment, I couldn't breathe. I never imagined such a tiny, simple gesture would make me feel such a rush of emotion. I looked down at her sweet, innocent face, her peach-fuzzy head, her sly little smile, and felt a rush of happiness and warmth and hope. Hope for me, hope for the future, hope for the whole world. I kissed her fingertips and she laughed. I laughed too and reluctantly handed her back to Lem.

I swear Sandy can sleep anywhere. I could prop him up in broom closet with a yappy puppy and he'd be snoring within 15 seconds. I, however, am the exact opposite. As he slept peacefully behind me in our darkened hotel room, I stood at the window and gazed across Manhattan, an ocean of lights and humanity spread out twelve stories below. My head buzzed with jet lag but I couldn't sleep. I still couldn't quite believe I was in New York City, standing in nothing but a t-shirt and panties, looking at the tri-colored top of the Empire State Building. Further back, the art-deco stacked arch of the Chrysler Building carved perfect triangular slices of light against the night sky. The soundproof hotel windows made me feel like I was watching a movie with the volume off. Yellow taxis streamed down the streets until the lights changed and they slowed and stopped, bottle-necking for a few moments and then then light changed back and the stream once again surged forward, picking people up and dispensing them again in other parts of the madly beautiful city. I leaned my forehead against the glass. I had long dreamed of visiting New York and now here I was, not as a tourist but as an artist. They had invited me here as an artist. I closed my eyes and nearly fell over from fatigue. Crawling under the blankets next to Sandy, I finally slept.

We had, at my insistence, arrived in New York two days before the show's opening so we had a little time to see the sights. On our first morning, we bundled ourselves into the warmest jackets we'd brought – September in New York is a whole lot different than September in California – and headed for the Metropolitan Museum of Art, stopping on the way for bagels and coffee.

"This is the single best bagel I've ever had in the whole of my life," Lem said, holding it aloft like an amazing treasure she'd just unearthed. A blob of cream cheese slipped from the bottom of it and landed squarely on Willow's head, sticking up from the snugglie strapped to Lem's front. The baby craned her head around and looked up at her mother. We all laughed, so Willow laughed too. River picked the blob off her head and gently rubbed the rest of it off with a napkin.

"You have been cream cheesed, little one," he said, kissing her fuzzy head. "Welcome to New York."

We walked while we ate and talked. The coffee was strong and hot, and Lem was right – the bagels alone were worth the trip.

"How much further is the museum?" Lem asked. "River's kid is getting heavier and heavier."

"It's all the cream cheese she's wearing," River said.

I laughed.

"I think we should just get in a cab," I said. "It's somewhere in Central Park and I have no idea how to get us there."

We tossed our trash into a nearby can and River went to the curb and stuck his arm out. Almost immediately, a cab pulled over.

"How did you know to do that?" I asked, amazed.

"I've been here a few times, visiting friends during college," he said, helping Lem into the backseat. "It's still just the luck of the draw if they're actually going to stop or not."

The taxi deposited us in front of an enormous gray building with columns taller and thicker than I'd ever seen.

"Oh my God," I whispered, looking up at it. "The Met. I can't believe I'm really here."

Sandy took my hand as I got out. We paid the suggested donation to get in – or rather, Sandy did. All I did was stare. It was the most amazing, impressive, utterly intimidating museum I'd ever seen. Sandy got a list of exhibits from a woman near the entrance and we wandered through the mezzanines, taking in each exhibit. After a stop in the café for a rest and some coffee and to let Lem nurse Willow, we resumed our exploration.

I had studied pictures of the Met, of course, and imagined what it would be like to have my work on display here, but the sheer size of it, the way the massive steps welcomed you like a stern professor whose very appearance let you know you'd better be taking all this seriously, was more daunting than I'd expected. Groups of school kids, glad enough just to be out of their classrooms, shoved each other and laughed. Graduate students in cargo pants and hipster glasses approached paintings and sculptures with an air of studious importance, notebooks or sketchpads in their hands. Paintings by Rembrandt, Picasso, Monet, O'Keeffe, Stieglitz hung on the walls. I stepped as close to Monet's "Water Lilies" as I dared, so close that the famous image blurred into individual brushstrokes. I caught my breath as I realized I was looking at ridges of paint actually left behind by the great master's brush. This wasn't a photo, this was real. I felt as though I were looking over his shoulder, watching the flowers move from his mind's eye to the canvas.

I was so absorbed in what I was seeing, I didn't realize the others had gone on until Sandy came back to find me. We had just come into Gallery 903 when I saw it. I stopped short and grabbed Sandy's hand and pointed.

"What?" he said, then followed where I was pointing. "Ohhhh. Look at that."

I had dropped his hand and was making my way toward Brancusi's "Bird in Space." I stood before it, unable to believe I was standing so close to one of his pieces. It was smooth, fluid, beautiful.

"Brancusi," Lem whispered from beside me.

"Yeah," I whispered back, feeling close to tears. "Brancusi."

"What's it made of?" she asked.

"Marble," I said. "Look at those lines. I've never known anyone who could make a complicated piece look so simple. He was an absolute genius."

The others quietly drifted away to look at other pieces in the gallery, leaving me alone in my reverie. I walked around the piece several times, slowly, my eyes traveling every inch of it, committing it to memory. To this day I can't figure out the mystique of Brancusi's method. His works do look simple. Even the eyes on his faces are not more than curved lines that just give the idea of the features. His piece "The Kiss" looks almost childlike in its simplicity, but I've tried to replicate it and believe me, there's nothing simple about it. Monet had moved me, but Brancusi was reaching into my very soul. He was here, or at least his work was, in New York. With mine. With me.

"Monsieur Brancusi," I whispered. "I am so nervous about my art opening. I'm not a real artist. Not like this. Not like you."

But as I stood there, gazing at "Bird in Space," I slowly felt the truth dawning on me, the truth everyone had tried to tell me but until that moment had been either unwilling or unable to see: I am an artist. I am. I could feel Brancusi smiling at me. I smiled back. Taking a deep breath, I went to join the others.

Coming Together and Falling Apart

The opening night reception was surreal. From the moment I walked past the fountain and through the doors of Lincoln Center, I felt like I was moving through a dream. Every time I caught sight of myself in my glittery, slinky black dress, I thought I was seeing someone else. Sandy and River were in tuxedos, which looked amazing although in truth I knew they both couldn't wait to be back in jeans. Lem was resplendent in a yellow satin dress, her hair in an updo that looked elegant even though it was purple. Willow was in red velvet dress, and on top of her head was a big red velvet bow she kept trying to pull off. The art was displayed tastefully all around, and we walked around for a little while, just soaking it all in. Uniformed waiters moved among the people with trays of hors d'oeuvres and glasses of champagne.

"Ms. Carson?" a man's voice came from my left and I turned to see a tall man in a dark gray tuxedo smiling down at me.

"Yes!"

"I'm David Kaplan, show curator."

"Oh yes! Hi, it's great meeting you." I shook his hand with my usual heartiness, then stopped myself and tried to be more sophisticated. "It's a pleasure to be here. I'm honored to have had my work selected. This is my husband, Sanford Moreland."

Mr. Kaplan smiled at me, showing two rows of absolutely perfect teeth. He smelled expensive.

"Have you seen your piece?" he asked. When I told him no, that we'd not long arrived, he offered to show me. My entourage trailing behind us, he led me past some truly amazing paintings, mixed-media sculptures, and photography, until we came to my piece. It looked small, much smaller than most of the other pieces I'd seen, but beautiful. It was perched on top of a column that reached almost to my chest, and was displayed on a piece of simple black fabric. All my anxiety vanished. It was a great piece. A damned great piece. I was an artist. I grabbed Sandy's hand and laughed.

"It looks great!" I said. "I'm an artist!"

Mr. Kaplan looked puzzled, but Sandy kissed my cheek.

"You're an artist," he said, squeezing me.

"Oh, here comes someone else I'd like you to meet," Mr. Kaplan said, motioning to someone behind me. "This is Adam Mossberg of the New York Foundation for the Arts."

"Pleased to meet you," Mr. Mossberg said, shaking my hand. "I was admiring your piece earlier. I'd love to hear more about it."

"I was about to ask the same thing." Another voice made me turn. "Hi, I'm Katie Fieldstone from the New York Times. I'm doing a piece on new artists at this show and I was just about to ask what Mr. Mossberg asked." She smiled at him. "Hi Adam."

"Katie, good to see you again."

"So tell us about your piece." She moved closer and squinted at it. "It's beautiful."

"Thank you. It's, well, it's a butterfly." I felt suddenly awkward and embarrassed, like she'd caught me naked with no excuse.

"And it's inside ... is that a cocoon?"

"Well, of a sort." I paused, unsure of how to explain. I looked up at Sandy, then at Lem and River, who were all smiling at me, then at Willow, who had finally succeeded in pulling the velvet ribbon off her head and was trying to eat it. I smiled through the fullness of my heart and turned back to the reporter who was watching me expectantly.

"It's everything," I said. "It's everything that has tried to keep the butterfly closed up. It's the world, it's society, it's hate and preju-dice and destructive behavior and negativity, it's all that we have created to seal our true selves off from each other and the world."

Her pen was flying back and forth across the paper. "And the but-terfly?"

"The butterfly is the soul of what's really happening underneath all of that," I said quietly, my eyes on my artwork. "We create these shells around ourselves, thinking we'll be safer that way, be-lieving that there is too much bad in the world and that if we let our real selves show, we'll be hurt. We think that no one else can possibly understand or accept us for who we really are, so we exist within the bubble, the shell we've built. And all around us, everyone else is living in their own little shell, keeping themselves and their beauty sealed off. We're waiting, we're all waiting, for someone to break open that first shell, to be who they really are, to spread their wings and take flight and say 'Here I am, now show me you.' And if we would all be willing to take that first step, to be that vulnerable, more people would follow, until the whole sky was filled with different colors and sizes and shapes, and the silent flutter of our wings would send the last of the shells scattering to the winds. And that would be..." I touched the top of my piece with my index finger, searching for the right word. "Perfect."

There was a split second of silence when I stopped speaking, and I heard a woman's voice from behind me.

"Ariel?"

I turned. It took me a moment to remember where I'd seen the gray-haired woman before. She was familiar – really familiar. Suddenly I realized she was the woman from the back row of my AA meeting. Only this time I was looking right into her face. My heart stopped for a moment. My voice was barely a whisper.

"Mom?"

The New York Times Gets One Hell of a Story

This was unreal. This couldn't be happening. The silence around us was deafening as even the reporter's pen stopped scratching. The woman and I were staring at each other, frozen on the spot. Finally, almost imperceptibly, she nodded. Then, when I didn't move, she nodded for real.

"Yes," she said. "It's me."

"Oh my God," I whispered. "Oh my God. I don't... I can't... oh my God."

I suddenly felt dizzy, and I reached for something to steady myself. I felt Sandy take my arm.

"I don't even know what to say right now," I said. "You. I can't believe you're here. I can't believe you're you. You're YOU, from the meetings, and now you're here, and what the HELL, Mom! I can't even... I can't even look at you right now. I'm so... I'm... shit!" I was afraid I was going to cry. "How dare you show up on the biggest night of my life? How dare you follow me and... spy on me... I haven't seen you since I was six years old and you just pick tonight to crash in on me?"

The reporter tapped me on the arm.

"I'm sorry but do you want me to go?"

"No," I told her. "Stay. You might as well stay since you've heard this much. You want a great story? Here's your great story. Artist's mom ruins the biggest night of her daughter's life after forty-year absence."

I looked around and noticed that everyone had stuck around for this nightmare of a family reunion. Mr. Mossberg, Mr. Kaplan, the reporter, everyone.

"Uh, well, this is... this is interesting," Mr. Kaplan cleared his throat. "I was going to introduce you, but it seems you already know each other. Ariel Carson, this is Susan Carson. She also has artwork in this show. Just down the row here, in fact. So ...

you're... mother and... daughter?"

She and I were still staring at each other. Finally she spoke.

"Yes," she said, turning to Mr. Kaplan. "Ariel is my daughter. She was raised by her father. We haven't seen each other since she was a very little girl."

"So wait... let me see if I've got this right," Katie Fieldstone said, holding up her reporter's notebook like a referee with a yellow card. "Ariel, you came to New York from San Francisco when your work was chosen for this show, never having had a piece shown in New York before. And Susan, you also have work here, and you didn't know that Ariel was going to be here too? And you haven't seen each other in forty years?"

"Yeah," I said quietly. "Something like that."

"That's most of it," my mother said. "In a nutshell."

"I can't get my head around this," Katie said.

"That makes two of us," I said.

"Look, this event is about to wind down for the night anyway, so would you all like to go someplace where you can talk?" Mr. Kaplan asked. "There's a coffee shop right down the street that generally isn't too busy at this time of night."

"Thank you," Sandy said. "That would be great. We really appreciate your help."

"Do you mind if I come?" Katie said. "I don't want to intrude, but this is just too good for me to pass up."

Sandy looked at me. I shrugged.

"You've got this much," I said. "You might as well get the whole story. What the hell do I care?" For all my pissed-off bravado, all I really wanted to do was get back on a plane and go back to San Francisco and hide under my bed for the rest of my life. Instead, the whole sordid family history that I'd always tried to distance myself from was about to play out in the New York Times. How appropriate.

Mr. Kaplan and Mr. Mossberg tactfully withdrew, and the rest of us headed in the direction he'd pointed us.

"Are you sure you don't want to be alone with your mother for awhile?" Sandy whispered in my ear once we were outside.

"I definitely do not want to be alone with her," I said. "I don't know who she is – she's a stranger to me."

"I can get rid of the reporter," he said. "You don't have to do this."

"If she leaves now, she'll only have half the story and it will probably end up worse," I whispered. "I seriously think she should stay at this point."

My head was still spinning as we all sat down in the cozy little shop that smelled comfortingly of coffee and pastry. Sandy ordered coffee all around. No one spoke. I couldn't even bring myself to look at my mother. Finally, Katie spoke.

"Well, uh, I don't really want to run this thing, but I am very interested to hear the whole story," she said "It isn't every day a feature on a new artist takes such an interesting turn."

I finally raised my eyes to once more look my mother in the face.

"Yes, Mother," I said. "Why don't you tell us the whole story? Starting with telling me where the hell you've been for the past forty years?" I could feel angry tears beginning to pick at the back of my eyes and I looked away. Unfortunately, my gaze landed on Lem and River. His arm was around her, and Willow was sleeping peacefully against her mother's chest. They were a family, a warm nest of love and safety where the little one could grow up knowing she was wanted and cherished. I felt like I was looking at a snapshot of all that had been taken from me. I could feel my hands shaking and I clenched them on my lap, not trusting myself to speak again.

"I didn't expect this whole reunion to play out in the press, but I guess since it's already started, we might as well," my mother said. "I left Ariel and her father when she was six years old. I just left, without telling anyone anything. I needed space. To think, to find myself. I'd married too quickly and I just never felt it was … right. He hadn't misrepresented himself in any way, my husband, but once I got to know him as he really was, I knew I'd made a mistake. But then I found out I was pregnant, so I stayed. I really did try. I had no idea how to be a mother, I hadn't even ever thought about whether I wanted children. I didn't know what to do – she was so tiny and so fragile and she was completely dependent on me. On me. And I could barely take care of myself, and now I was responsible for this tiny, precious life. So I just followed whatever my husband did. He seemed to have it all under control, so I let him do the parenting and I just sort of followed his lead."

I was gripping my coffee cup so hard I was afraid I might break it. I didn't speak, didn't look at her. Sandy's hand resting on my leg felt like the only thing keeping me moored.

"So what made you decide to leave?" Katie asked gently.

"I don't know that I ever really did make a conscious decision," she answered. "At least not a pre-meditated decision. One day, Ariel came home from school and I fixed the after-school snack I was always supposed to give her, and I looked at her sitting there at the table, with our well-ordered life all around us, and I suddenly could see that we were both serving a life sentence in a room with no windows." She brushed away a tear that had been sneaking down her cheek. "So I left. I didn't want her to grow up to be as lost and hopeless as I was. I figured if I left, she'd have a chance."

"Bull SHIT," I burst out. "You left me there with Dad because you didn't want the responsibility of marriage and motherhood. You weren't saving me, so you can just skip the sob story. You weren't out to save anyone but yourself."

She met my gaze levelly.

"You're right," she said. "I was out to save myself. But I didn't know how else to save you. If you'd grown any older watching your mother fumble around and just do whatever her husband said, what kind of an example would that have been? You'd never have had a normal relationship with a man. And I wasn't sure I was strong enough to be a good example for you if I'd taken you with me. I was a mess, Ariel. I was just a stupid kid, trapped by marriage, and scared to death of motherhood. It wasn't that I didn't want you, my little one, I did want you. I didn't expect to get pregnant, no, but I wanted you more than anything. The problem is that as you grew, I was worried I was doing you more harm than good. Your father is a good man – a little odd in his thinking and routines, but he would never have hurt you. He loved you so much that I knew you'd be safe with him, and that your life would make more sense to you than it would if your flighty, flaky mother was still around."

"You took the Fig Newtons."

There was a moment of silence and out of nowhere, my mother laughed.

"Yes," she said. "I did."

"You took the Fig Newtons?" Katie interrupted. "What does that mean?"

"It means she took the Fig Newtons," I said. "She gave me three and she took the rest of the package when she left. It was a new package too." I looked back at my mother. "To this day, I hoard Fig Newtons."

"Yeah," she said. "So do I."

Katie was scribbling furiously in her notebook. I couldn't imagine what kind of a story she was going to get out of this. Maybe the New York Times had a "Domestic Train Wrecks" section. Well if not, they would now.

"So you're both artists," she said, looking up. "Did you know that?"

"I didn't know she was," I said. "My father never mentioned it."

"He didn't know," my mother said. "I picked it up a few years after I left."

"What kind of art?" Katie asked.

"I paint in watercolor," my mother said.

"I sculpt," I added. "In clay mostly, but some wood." I was relieved beyond reason that she wasn't a sculptor.

"So tell me how you happened to be in the same show, in New York, which is especially interesting given that you both live in San Francisco. Right?"

The waitress refilled everyone's coffee, causing a momentary distraction, and when she was gone, I busied myself putting way too much sugar in my cup to avoid having to answer.

"Well, this is where the story gets kind of personal," my mother said. "Ariel, do you mind if I tell her about... the meetings?"

I shrugged.

"It's all out there now anyway," I said. "Go ahead."

"When I left, I wasn't sure where I was going to go," she explained. "I'd always loved San Francisco and I didn't want to go far, so I found a place in Sausalito. I was careful to avoid certain places in San Francisco as I didn't want to risk running into Ariel or her father. I was dying to know how you were getting along, Ariel, but I didn't want to disrupt your life at that point."

"So thoughtful," I muttered. Sandy squeezed my leg a little harder than necessary and I scowled at him.

"I was still battling my old demons, and some others that had come up along the way," she paused and seemed to be struggling for the right words. "Like booze. I'd always enjoyed a drink now and then, but I started to depend on alcohol to get me through every day, and one night I finally felt like I'd hit rock bottom, so I found an AA meeting that was far enough from where I lived I figured I wouldn't see anyone I knew. I sat in the back for a few weeks and didn't say anything, didn't talk to anyone. And one night..." she stopped to swipe away more tears. "I heard a woman's voice from the front say her name was Ariel. And when I looked up, I knew I was looking at my little girl. I couldn't stop crying. I didn't want to believe my baby had the same drinking problem I did." By now she was sobbing. Lem, who was also weeping, handed her some napkins from the dispenser. Once she was back under control, she continued.

"A few meetings later, Ariel was sharing about her work being chosen for this juried art show in New York, and I was pretty sure it had to be the same show, as I'd just gotten my own notification. I wasn't going to say anything to you, Ariel, I wasn't going to even talk to you at the show because I knew you probably wouldn't want to see me, but I overheard what you were saying about your piece, about the butterfly, and it was just so beautiful I couldn't stay away anymore. I wanted you to know that..." she stopped and struggled to speak through her sobs. "That I'm proud of you."

Goodbye Again

It felt weird, saying goodbye to my mother. I didn't have the chance to say it the first time, and this time we hadn't ever really said hello, and now it was goodbye again. We were standing at her departure gate at JFK Airport, as her flight was boarding. Ours was boarding from a different gate an hour later. She was making a stop in Kansas City and another in Seattle before heading back to Sausalito, she told me. After a long night of talking, even after the reporter was gone and Lem, River and Sandy were in bed, we reached a place of, if not exactly peace, of mutual understanding, and the good and bad of each other. She was still a stranger, but one who was now vaguely familiar to me, and her place in my history was more in focus than it had ever been.

"I'll call you," she said, hugging me. As I hugged her back, I could feel her slip something into my shoulder bag. She handed her ticket to the agent, turning to wave once more before disappearing down the jetway. I stood for a moment, watching the spot I'd last seen her.

"No, you won't," I said quietly. "Goodbye, Mom."

Taking a deep breath, I went back to where Sandy was sitting with Lem and River. Willow, sitting on River's lap, was sucking her thumb and touching his beard with her other hand. They had decided not to stay on in New York any longer but to head back to California with us instead. River had said he had gotten a call for a big landscaping job, but I suspected Lem wanted to stay close to me.

"Are you okay?" Sandy asked me.

"Yeah," I said. "I will be." Lem jumped up and threw her arms around me.

"Oh Ari, what a trip. I sense that you're feeling very confused and fragmented right now." She looked up at me earnestly, her wide, innocent eyes completely without guile. I laughed and then started to cry. I hugged her, hard. This was my family now, every last one of them.

"That is exactly how I'm feeling," I said. "Your gift never ceases to amaze me."

I sat down beside Sandy and reached into my bag for a tissue. My hand bumped something that made a crinkling sound and I pulled out a package of Fig Newtons. On top was a sticky note: "I took three – the rest are for you."

Epilogue

Katie's article came out in the New York Times two days after we got back to San Francisco – giving me just enough time to warn my father about it and tell him the whole story. Surprisingly, he seemed to take it all in stride. He's gotten a lot mellower since Meredith came into his life. He still internalizes a lot, though, so we'll see what happens.

In case you're wondering, yes – it was a great article. She talked about me as an artist, about my early life, how I'd started sculpting as an escape without any real aspirations to do it professionally, about the juried show, my trip to New York, my mother's unexpected appearance... all in all, it was probably one of the best human interest stories I've ever read, and I don't just say that because it was about me. Well, maybe a little. Even Brancusi got a mention.

In the months since the article appeared, I've been commissioned to do a series of sculptures for a wealthy New York woman who wants her family's history "set in stone," as she put it, and asked to participate in another show in New York next spring. I also got a call a few days ago from the head of the San Francisco Botanical Garden to ask if I'll create a sculpture fountain for a new section of the garden. River is going to be handling the landscape design and all the planting, and I'm really looking forward to working with him.

Ralph and Ellen are getting married next weekend and I've tried to figure out how to get out of going, but I'm pretty sure I'm stuck. Oh well. I really do like her, and since he and I made some semblance of peace, he's been a little more tolerable. Don't get me wrong – I still think she could do a lot better than him, but hey. Whatever blows her tutu up.

Oh, and Lem and River are having another baby. She's not due for eight and a half months, but she says this one is a boy.

Author's Note

Although releasing live butterflies at weddings is a well-meant practice and one that has gained popularity in recent years, during the course of my research for this book, I've learned that it isn't the best idea.

Many places sell lab-raised butterflies for just such occasions. They're shipped all over the country, and often released in areas that are not native to their particular species. This brings a host of problems, including the potential for spreading disease to other butterflies, and interference with the butterflies' natural migratory paths. Two more issues: often these butterflies arrive dead or nearly dead, and the practice of purchasing commercially-obtained butterflies means a bigger demand which leads to a problem with – you guessed it – poachers.

As part of my research, I've been talking with Dr. Jeffrey Glassberg, president of the North American Butterfly Association, and he has told me that the NABA supports legislation being considered by the City of San Francisco that would ban the release of commercially-obtained butterflies for these reasons and more.

The butterflies that Ariel released at Lem's wedding were not commercially raised. The environmentally-conscious Cora simply collects local caterpillars to help keep them safe from pesticides and other hazards, then releases the butterflies once they're ready. These are the butterflies that Ariel released at Lem's wedding. We all know that Lem wouldn't approve of anything else.

www.ingramcontent.com/pod-product-compliance
Lightning Source LLC
Chambersburg PA
CBHW030613130626
46552CB00002B/549